Rowe is a paranorn

Praise for Not Quite Dead

"[Rowe] has penned a winner with *Not Quite Dead*, the first novel in her new NightHunter vampire series...an action-packed, sensual, paranormal romance that will captivate readers from the outset... Brimming with vampires, danger, resurrection, Louisiana bayou, humor, surprising plot twists, fantasy, romance and love, this story is a must-read!" ~ *Romance Junkies:*

Praise for Darkness Possessed

"A story that will keep you on the edge of your seat, and characters you won't soon forget!" - Paige Tyler, *USA Today* Bestselling Author of the X-OPS Series

"*Darkness Possessed*...is an action-packed, adrenaline pumping paranormal romance that will keep you on the edge of your seat... Suspense, danger, evil, life threatening situations, magic, hunky Calydons, humor, fantasy, mystery, scorching sensuality, romance, and love – what more could you ask for in a story? Readers – take my advice – do not miss this dark, sexy tale!" ~ *Romance Junkie*s

---

Praise for Darkness Unleashed

"Once more, award winning author Stephanie Rowe pens a winner with *Darkness Unleashed*, the seventh book in her amazing Order of the Blade series...[an] action-packed, sensual story that will keep you perched on the edge of your seat, eagerly turning pages to discover the outcome…one of the best paranormal books I have read this year." *~Dottie, Romancejunkies.com*

Praise for Forever in Darkness

"Stephanie Rowe has done it again. The Order Of The Blade series is one of the best urban fantasy/paranormal series I have read. Ian's story held me riveted from page one. It is sure to delight all her fans. Keep them coming!" ~ *Alexx Mom Cat's Gateway Book Blog*

Praise for Darkness Awakened

"A fast-paced plot with strong characters, blazing sexual tension and sprinkled with witty banter, Darkness Awakened sucked me in and kept me hooked until the very last page." ~ *Literary Escapism*

"Rarely do I find a book that so captivates my attention, that makes me laugh out loud, and cry when things look bad. And the sex, wow! It took my breath away... The pace kept me on the edge of my seat, and turning the pages. I did not want to put this book down... [Darkness Awakened] is a must read." ~ D. Alexx Miller, Alexx Mom Cat's Gateway Book Blog

Praise for Darkness Seduced

"[D]ark, edgy, sexy … sizzles on the page…sex with soul shattering connections that leave the reader a little breathless!...Darkness Seduced delivers tight plot lines, well written, witty and lyrical - Rowe lays down some seriously dark and sexy tracks. There is no doubt that this series will have a cult following. " ~ *Guilty Indulgence Book Club*

"I was absolutely enthralled by this book…heart stopping action fueled by dangerous passions and hunky, primal men…If you're looking for a book that will grab hold of you and not let go until it has been totally devoured, look no further than Darkness Seduced."~*When Pen Met Paper Reviews*

Praise for Darkness Surrendered

"Book three of the Order of the Blades series is…superbly original and excellent, yet the passion, struggle and the depth of emotion that Ana and Elijah face is so brutal, yet is also pretty awe inspiring. I was swept away by Stephanie's depth of character detail and emotion. I absolutely loved the roller-coaster that Stephanie, Ana and Elijah took me on." ~ *Becky Johnson, Bex 'n' Books!*

"Darkness Surrendered drew me so deeply into the story that I felt Ana and Elijah's emotions as if they were my own…they completely engulfed me in their story…Ingenious plot turns and edge of your seat suspense…make Darkness Surrendered one of the best novels I have read in years." ~*Tamara Hoffa, Sizzling Hot Book Reviews*

Praise for Ice

"*Ice*, by Stephanie Rowe, is a thrill ride!" ~ Lisa Jackson, #1 *New York Times* bestselling author

"Passion explodes even in the face of spiraling danger as Rowe offers a chilling thrill-ride through a vivid--and unforgiving--Alaskan wilderness." ~ Cheyenne McCray, *New York Times* bestselling author

"*Ice* delivers pulse-pounding chills and hot romance as it races toward its exciting climax!" ~ JoAnn Ross, *New York Times* bestselling author

"Stephanie Rowe explodes onto the romantic suspense scene with this edgy, sexy and gripping thriller. From the very first page, the suspense is chilling, and there's enough sizzling passion between the two main characters to melt the thickest arctic ice. Get ready for a tense and dangerous adventure." ~ *Fresh Fiction*

"Stephanie Rowe makes her entry into Romantic Suspense, and what an awesome entry! From the very first pages to the end, heart-stopping danger and passion grab the heart. ... sends shivers down the spine... magnificent... mind-chilling suspense... riveting... A wonderful romance through and through!" ~ *Merrimon Book Reviews*

"[a] thrilling entry into romantic suspense... Rowe comes through with crackling tension as the killer closes in." ~ *Publisher's Weekly*

▨▨▨▨

Praise for Chill

"*Chill* is a riveting story of danger, betrayal, intrigue and the healing powers of love… *Chill* has everything a reader needs – death, threats, thefts, attraction and hot, sweet romance." ~ Jeanne Stone Hunter, *My Book Addiction Reviews*

"Once again Rowe has delivered a story with adrenalin-inducing action, suspense and a dark edged hero that will melt your heart and send a chill down your spine." ~ Sharon Stogner, *Love Romance Passion*

"*Chill* packs page turning suspense with tremendous emotional impact. Buy a box of Kleenex before you read *Chill*, because you will definitely need it! ...*Chill* had a wonderfully complicated plot, full of twist and turns. " ~ Tamara Hoffa, *Sizzling Hot Book Reviews*

▨▨▨▨

Praise for No Knight Needed

"*No Knight Needed* is m-a-g-i-c-a-l! Hands down, it is one of the best romances I have read. I can't wait till it comes out and I can tell the world about it." ~*Sharon Stogner, Love Romance Passion*

"*No Knight Needed* is contemporary romance at its best....There was not a moment that I wasn't completely engrossed in the novel, the story, the characters. I very audibly cheered for them and did not shed just one tear, nope, rather bucket fulls. My heart at times broke for them. The narrative and dialogue surrounding these 'tender' moments in particular were so beautifully crafted, poetic even; it was this that had me blubbering. And of course on the flip side of the heart-wrenching events, was the amazing, witty humour....If it's not obvious by now, then just to be clear, I love this book! I would most definitely and happily reread, which is an absolute first for me in this genre." *~Becky Johnson, Bex 'N' Books*

"*No Knight Needed* is an amazing story of love and life...I literally laughed out loud, cried and cheered.... *No Knight Needed* is a must read and must re-read." *~Jeanne Stone-Hunter, My Book Addiction Reviews*

Shadows of Darkness

ISBN 10: 194096816X

ISBN 13: 9781940968162

Copyright © 2015 by Stephanie Rowe.

Cover design ©2015 MJC Imageworks. For more info on the cover artist, please visit www.mjcimageworks.com.

Acknowledgements

Special thanks to my beta readers, who always work incredibly hard under tight deadlines to get my books read. I appreciate so much your willingness to tell me when something doesn't work! I treasure your help, and I couldn't do this without you. Hugs to you all!

There are so many to thank by name, more than I could count, but here are those who I want to called out specially for all they did to help this book come to life: Leslie Barnes, Kayla Bartley, Alencia Bates Salters, Alyssa Bird, Jean Bowden, Shell Bryce, Kelley Daley Curry, Holly Collins, Ashley Cuesta, Denise Fluhr, Sandi Foss, Valerie Glass, Christina Hernandez, Heidi Hoffman, Jeanne Stone, Rebecca Johnson, Dottie Jones, Janet Juengling-Snell, Deb Julienne, Bridget Koan, Felicia Low, Phyllis Marshall, Suzanne Mayer, Erin McRae, Jodi Moore, Ashlee Murphy, Judi Pflughoeft, Carol Pretorius, Kasey Richardson, Karen Roma, Caryn Santee, Summer Steelman, Regina Thomas, and Linda Watson.

Special thanks to Michael James Canalas at MJC Imageworks for a wonderful cover. Mom, you're the best. It means so much that you believe in me. I love you. Special thanks also to my amazing, beautiful, special daughter, who I love more than words could ever express. You are my world, sweet girl, in all ways.

Dedication

This book is dedicated to Deborah Berman, who is the most amazing human being I have ever met.

Shadows

of

Darkness

An *Order of the Blade* Novel

Stephanie

Rowe

Chapter 1

Levi Hart froze, his senses shocked into hyper-awareness when he caught the unmistakable scent of a *woman*. It plunged past his shields, invading his being with a force so strong he had no chance to protect himself from the sheer intensity of her presence. He swore and went utterly still. His mind went into hyper-focus as he fought to regain control, his body barely swaying on the ancient meat hook he'd been chained to for over a century.

But with each breath he took, the fragile, delicate scent of pure femininity wrapped itself tighter around him. Hot. Sensual. Tempting. And utterly dangerous to a Calydon warrior who was driven by a dark, powerful need for a woman.

His ancient instincts rose fast and hard, a driving lust that he hadn't succumbed to in centuries. Swearing under his breath, he closed his eyes, summoning what was left of his once formidable discipline to regain control of his body and his senses. It took precious seconds to shut down the lust burning through him. He had to engage strength he couldn't afford to waste in order to crush the almost insurmountable need to find her *right then*, but he did it.

The relief was instant, but a residue of emptiness resonated through him, as if his very being was stumbling in the absence of that sexual hunger. Without the distraction, however, a sharp-edged focus settled over him. He narrowed his eyes and called upon his preternatural senses, sending waves of psychic energy out into the surrounding tunnels, searching for the physical presence of the woman he had scented.

He found nothing.

A dark fury raged through him, anger that he couldn't find her. Urgency mounted, and he sent out another wave of energy, but this time, he opened his mind, sending the tentacles of his consciousness out into the air, searching with ruthless speed. Within seconds, he picked up her feminine energy again. This time, he kept his physical response contained, and he allowed his mind to hurtle toward her at a mind-numbing pace, racing through tunnels and around corners, faster and faster, gaining speed with each millisecond, her scent becoming stronger and stronger until—

He found her.

The moment his mind touched hers, she sucked in her breath, and her mind snapped to his, injecting warmth and passion into his cold, isolated being. His entire body clenched in response, and tension radiated through his muscles as he fought to concentrate. She smelled of spring and outdoors, of grass, of nature, and of a lazy sensuality, things he hadn't experienced in over a hundred years. But since he'd opened his mind to her, it wasn't simply her physical being he accessed. Her emotions assaulted him, a dizzying onslaught of fear, courage, and desperation, all of it ruthlessly contained by her single-minded focus and determination. His name reverberated through her mind, and it was layered through her entire being.

All her attention was centered on *him.*

His body responded to the knowledge, a tightening of his cock that he couldn't control no matter how hard he fought it. To have his name and his existence so intricately woven into the fabric of her being was so visceral that he could almost feel her presence, as if she was right in front of him. He couldn't keep his physical response contained, and his lust spilled over their connection into her. Instantly, desire flooded her, and he felt her body respond to his.

The connection between them was electric and intense, igniting his cells like fire licking its way through his body. He was a cold-blooded assassin who'd spent a lifetime honing his utter lack of emotion and eradicating his need for physical connection with a woman, and yet, in mere seconds, she'd stripped away every last defense and created a need in him so powerful he knew he'd be sprinting through the tunnels in search of her if he weren't locked down.

Who the hell was she? And why was she there? No one had set foot in any of the caverns surrounding his prison since he'd been chained up, and he didn't believe it was a coincidence that she was so close, thousands of feet below the surface of the earth in tunnels that no human being would ever stumble across, thinking about him. *Who are you?* He pressed the question at her, instinctively erecting a telepathic bridge between their minds.

She froze in response, and for a split second, he felt her confusion that he was speaking in her mind. Then fear rippled through her, and she slammed up her mental shields, severing their link. Emptiness assaulted him at the lack of connection, and he swore, struggling to regain his equilibrium. She'd cut him off, but he knew she'd heard him.

She'd heard him. After more than a century of complete isolation, *she'd heard him.* The sudden shock of having his existence recognized by another living creature hit him with an almost violent crash of emotion. His entire being suddenly burned with a need to be acknowledged, to be recognized, to be *seen.*

He shoved aside the emotions before they had a chance to claim him. He'd lived his whole life alone. He'd been a shadow in the night, a phantom who was everyone's worst nightmare. His solitary existence had never bothered him, not even for an instant, and he wasn't going to let it start grating on him now just because he'd been strung up like a carcass for a century and had scented a woman so enticing it could drive him mad if he let it consume him.

Her essence became stronger, and he realized she was headed right for him, on a direct path through the tunnels. *She was seeking him out.* Anticipation burned through him, an escalating need to see her, to hear her voice, to drag her against him and taste her mouth against his.

He swore and closed his eyes, raising his own shields to block her scent so he could recalibrate. What the hell? Why was he reacting like that to her? Was it just because he'd been isolated for so long? Or maybe she was some sort of seductress? Not that it mattered. He didn't want to make out with her. He wanted to *escape*.

This might be his chance.

He took a deep breath, summoning the combat-focus that had once been as instinctual as breathing and staying alive. Decades of no food, no water, and no external stimulation had weakened him, and his mind fought against his commands to concentrate so intently.

With a snarl of fury, he forced his mind to respond, channeling what was left of his strength into his mind until it coalesced into the razor-sharp clarity that had once defined him.

Straining to see in the darkness, he scanned the cave that had been his prison for so long. It had taken years for his eyes to adjust to the rampant darkness enough for him to be able to see anything, and even now, he could make out only the faintest dark shapes that indicated tunnel openings, escape routes that were only yards away, and yet completely out of reach.

She was in one of those tunnels, getting closer with each step.

Manipulating his body weight with the effortless grace of a man who'd spent countless hours figuring out how to stay fit and strong even while he was suspended by his wrists in a frigid, underground cave, Levi spun in a circle. He systematically inspected every inch of his cave, searching for indications that would tell him which direction she was approaching from.

Unable to resist the temptation, he inhaled again, and her scent wrapped around him, diffusing through his cells like a tendril of sunshine in a body that had long been dead. Energy pulsed through him, a sense of vitality he hadn't felt in decades. He reached out to her again, this time searching the space around her for more information on who she was. With his attention no longer only on her, he noticed the presence of two powerful males flanking her.

His hands clenched, and his muscles went taut. *She was with two Calydon warriors.* Possessiveness surged through him, a sudden fear for her safety. Was she their prisoner? Were they going to lock her up the way he'd been strung up? Suddenly, it was no longer about sex. It was no longer about his need to be acknowledged. It became only about protecting her. *Are you in danger?* He pressed the question ruthlessly at her mind, shattering her mental shields.

Again, she flinched, clearly hearing him, but once again, she didn't answer. Instead, she thrust him out of her mind as efficiently as he'd penetrated it.

He had to admit, he was impressed with her defenses, but at the same time, it was annoying as hell. He had no idea what the situation was. Did he need to protect her? Was she in danger?

No. No. *No.*

His job wasn't to protect *anyone.* He had one last mission to accomplish, and he couldn't afford to get distracted by a woman. He had to escape, hunt down the man who had nearly destroyed Levi's soul…and then kill him. He could allow the approaching threesome to mean only one thing to him: a chance to gain his freedom.

He steeled himself against the distraction of the woman, instead focusing on the men accompanying her. They moved with the lethal dangerousness he recognized as the trademark of the members of the Order of the Blade. The Order was an elite team of Calydon warriors whose mission was to defend innocents from rogue Calydons who had succumbed to their demon heritage and turned into mindless, slaughtering rogues. The Order members were ruthless in their quest, dripping with honor, trapped by their need to save strangers no matter what the cost to themselves.

No Order of the Blade member had ever bothered with him. Yeah, he wasn't one of the good guys, but he wasn't rogue, so they left him alone. Until now. What the hell was going on?

He had only moments until they emerged into his cavern. He could afford no mistakes.

After a hundred years of being suspended by his wrists, he was a fraction of the warrior he had once been. Despite his best efforts to keep his muscle tone, he wasn't even sure he'd be able to keep his balance when his feet finally touched down. His only chance to defeat them was to prevent them from challenging him to a fight he was too weak to win.

He flexed his muscles and pulled himself up so his head

was level with his wrists, activating his muscles. He shifted his weight, making the meat hook begin to sway like a pendulum. The arc got bigger and bigger, until he could hit the wall. He braced his feet against the cave and pushed off hard, working his legs, preparing his body. He pushed off the opposite wall, continuing to spin around so he could scan each entrance—

There! He finally tracked them, and he knew which tunnel they would be emerging from.

He spun to face the southwest opening, using his body weight and years of practice to regain control of his momentum and stop the swaying. His entire body was activated and ready, and his mind was clear, as centuries of experience in fighting for his life came back to him.

He studied the dark opening, his mind alert. There was no one to see, but he knew the trio was there, just out of his sight. Did they think he was so weak he couldn't sense them? "Show yourselves," he commanded.

For a moment, nothing happened, and then a blue light filled the cavern. Excruciating pain shot through Levi's eyes at the sudden brightness, and he instinctively turned his head into his arm to shield his eyes. Shit. He'd been in darkness so long that he couldn't even handle light.

"Are you Levi Hart?" A man asked the question, his voice low and controlled.

Fuck the man. Levi wanted to hear the woman's voice. Blinking against the pain in his eyes, Levi lifted his head higher, keeping his eyes shut against the blue light. "Who are you? All of you?" His voice scraped across his throat, rusty from decades of non-use. Adrenaline began to flow, ancient survival instincts that made the weapons branded on his forearms burn with the need for him to call them forth into his hands and into battle.

But he couldn't call them out. The chains that bound him wrapped all the way around his forearms, the treated metal efficiently negating his ability to call out the very weapons that defined him as a Calydon warrior. All he had were his feet, and his intelligence.

The man spoke again. "My name is Rohan. I have a deal for you."

"I don't make deals." Even with his eyes closed, the pain

was agonizing. Levi buried his face in his arm again, trying to protect his eyes. Shit. He was at such a disadvantage, fucking helpless. "Turn the light off," he commanded. "Now."

The light didn't decrease.

Then another man spoke, his voice less hard and brutal, laced with an irreverence that Levi didn't recall ever hearing in an Order member's voice. "For hell's sake, Rohan, stop being a show-off. You look like you're overcompensating for some sort of masculine shortcoming that the rest of us don't want to know about. Give the man a hug and a beer, and let's swap campfire stories instead of trying to blind the guy. He'll need his sight to help us, you know?"

"You're irritating as hell, Thano." Rohan said, but the light went out and the cave subsided into darkness.

Levi's body shuddered in relief, and the pain decreased significantly.

"I'm insightful and brilliant," Thano replied, with undaunted cheerfulness. "The fact you find it irritating reflects your own lack of brotherly love, not any shortcomings on my part. You're lucky to have me on your team, and you know it."

"Shut up." But there was a lack of harshness in Rohan's voice, and Levi realized they were a well-oiled duo.

Something shifted inside him at the bond between the warriors, an emotion he didn't recognize. He couldn't remember ever having that kind of camaraderie with anyone. He'd always scoffed at it. He'd considered it a weakness, but there was something about the banter between Rohan and Thano that made the darkness inside him seem even greater than it already was.

He wanted to see them. All of them. Thano. Rohan. *And the woman.*

Levi opened his eyes, but he could see nothing. His eyes were damaged from the light, robbing him of what little advantage he'd had in the darkness. Gritting his teeth, he ignored the searing pain in his eyes and continued to stare, trying to get his eyes to function again. Gradually, too slowly for his own satisfaction, his eyes began to recover. At first, all he could see were varying shades of darkness, but then he began to discern shapes.

He could see the outlines of the two warriors, one of which appeared to be riding a massive horse that, strangely, Levi had not sensed. Both men were tall and broad, with shoulders that indicated Levi was going to be pathetically overmatched if it came down to a fight before he had an opportunity to regain his strength.

But where was the woman? He couldn't see her, and he wanted to. He *needed to.*

The mounted warrior saluted him. "My name's Thano Savakis," he said, and Levi realized that he was one who'd seemed to find humor in the situation. "I'm honored to meet you, Levi. You're a serious badass."

Levi frowned at the salute. No one had ever respected him. Ever.

"I concur," Rohan said. "Your feats are legendary." Rohan seemed to hum with the kind of lethal energy that Levi recognized instantly as a formidable opponent.

Levi's eyes continued to adjust, and he could make out more details. Rohan's upper body was covered in a hooded cloak that hid his face from view. He was a warrior in his prime, and his energy was ruthlessly shrouded, a warrior in complete control. In his hand was a sword, the blade of which was glowing with the faintest trace of blue light, as if that had been the source of the flash of light.

Levi frowned at the blue electricity crackling over Rohan's blade. He'd heard of that sword. It was legendary, with powers far beyond that of an ordinary Calydon weapon. It had mystical magic that had evoked numerous tales about its power. It was the kind of weapon that would be able to slide through Levi's bonds and free him.

Anticipation rolled through Levi, and he could almost taste freedom. The appearance of that blue blade changed everything. Even though the metal that bound Levi had special properties designed to combat Calydon weapons, Rohan could free him with one strike, which meant he was a man worth negotiating with, not fighting against. "What do you want?" Levi asked. And where was the woman? He still hadn't been able to discern even her outline, but her scent was permeating the air like an invisible caress sliding across his flesh.

"Your skills live beyond you," Rohan said. "Very few impress me. You do."

Levi narrowed his eyes as the meaning of the Calydon's words sank in. He realized Rohan wanted Levi to kill someone for him. That was why the group had sought him out. They wanted him to assassinate someone that no one else could kill.

The deal became immediately apparent. Rohan would release Levi if he would become his own personal assassin. Bitterness spewed through Levi, and he shook his head. Freedom was not worth that price. "Never again." He would rather rot in his hell than *ever* become another man's pawn, or revisit that never-ending cycle of the deadly cravings that overtook him, inducing him to kill. It had taken almost thirty years of not feeding on another soul before Levi had begun to regain his sanity and his self-control, and he knew he couldn't risk it again. "I don't do that anymore."

Correction: there was one more man to kill, the man who'd controlled Levi for so long, who unleashed the monster within him. He had to be killed before he kidnapped other young boys and forced them into the life that had trapped Levi. The only flaw with Levi's plan, the problem he hadn't been able to sort out, was the fact that if he killed the bastard, it would turn Levi back into the monster that it had taken three decades to escape from. Levi was impossible to kill, blessed with an ability to heal from anything, even decapitation, which meant that if he lost his mind again…no one would be able to stop him. If Levi was caught in the killing thrall again, without specific targets to assassinate, he knew it was very likely he would find his own targets, and they might be innocents.

He had to find a way to protect the world from who he would become if he killed his former master. He would allow no one else to die at his hands. *No one.* There had to be a way, and he would find it. The first step was freedom, but not at the cost of killing anyone else. "I'm not for hire," he repeated. "I'm not an assassin anymore."

"I don't need you to kill anyone," Rohan said. "I need you to keep someone alive."

Levi went very still at the words, searching for the clue as to what Rohan really wanted. "I don't believe you," he said in a low voice. "I don't keep people alive. You know that." He still couldn't see the woman. Was she standing behind the men? *Come out. I want to see you.*

She didn't respond, and her shields held tight against him. What the hell? Why was he so driven to see her? And why was she blocking him? Then he had another thought. Why could he even communicate with her telepathically? It had felt so natural that he hadn't even thought about questioning it. But it was impossible. A Calydon's telepathic ability only worked with other Calydons…and with his *sheva*, the soulmate destined to destroy him.

Holy crap. *No.* Impossible. He had made a point of being impervious to the lure of his soulmate. He was unreachable. There was no way the woman before him was his *sheva*. *You're a telepath,* he said to her. *A siren and a telepath.* It made sense. Yes, Calydons could use their powers to communicate telepathically only with other Calydons and their soulmates, but plenty of other supernatural beings had that skill as well.

She wasn't his *sheva*. Just a sinful temptation with an impressive mind. Nothing for him to bother with.

Rohan shifted slightly, drawing Levi's attention. "Yes, I do know you kill people. And that's why you're the only one capable of this task. You're the only one I trust."

Trust? Levi almost laughed. Most people who had made the mistake of trusting him had ended up dead. "You lie."

"No. I have a lot at stake, and I can't afford a mistake." Rohan walked up to him, putting himself inches from Levi's bare feet, within easy striking distance.

Levi went still, watching Rohan carefully, knowing that he wasn't going to let Rohan walk away. Rohan had come into his personal space, and Levi was the only one who controlled it. But he would wait to attack. He never struck first, unless he had to. If there was a way to negotiate for his freedom, he'd give Rohan that chance before taking him down.

"Here's the deal," Rohan said. "I'll cut you down and free you. In return, you'll take an oath to the Order of the Blade and swear fealty to me. You'll do one task for me, and then you'll be free to do as you wish, unless I need assistance at some point in the future, at which point I can call on you."

Levi raised his brows. "I don't work for anyone. *Ever.*" The thought of being bound to another man made sweat trickle down his temple, but he kept his face impassive. "Cut me down and then I won't hurt you. That's the deal."

"I offer you freedom."

"I'll take the freedom myself." Levi closed his burned-out eyes, channeling all his energy into his remaining senses. He knew exactly where Rohan was, and where that sword was. "I'm not interested." He calculated swiftly what his move had to be to get the sword and cut his hands free. "But if you have cake, I'll take some of that. I miss cake." One. Two. Thr—

And then she spoke. It was only one word, one simple word, but it was enough. "Wait."

Her voice was like the music he remembered from the one time he'd gone into a church so many centuries ago. It was pure and beautiful, so rich with life that he felt like the entire world was glowing with a bright sunlight that would never penetrate the thickness of the shadows surrounding him. But somehow, her voice seemed to touch him, filtering through the layers of filth and grime on his soul, brushing over him like a seductive, delicate touch of something far more beautiful and pure than he had any right to experience.

His eyes snapped open just as she slid off the horse, where she'd apparently been riding behind Thano. It was too dark to see her clearly. All he could see were the soft waves of her hair, and she was wearing some sort of long coat that obscured the shape of her body. Frustration roared through him, a searing need to see her, to feel her, to touch her.

"Stay back," Rohan held out his hand to block her. "We don't know if he's safe yet."

Safe? He turned his attention back to Rohan, disgusted by the accusation. He might have killed innumerable people, but he'd always directed it at his targets. He'd never gone after an innocent. *Ever.* And now that he was sane, it really wasn't going to happen. "You—"

"No," she said. "I'm safe with him. I can tell."

Levi caught his breath as she walked up, coming to stand right beside Rohan. She was so close he could have grabbed her with his legs, but he didn't move. His eyes burned from straining so hard to discern her features, but it was just too damned dark. So, he simply waited.

"My name is Maya Brennan," she said. "I'm the one who needs help. I need you to get me safely to my destination. Rohan and Thano believe you can keep me alive. Will you help me?"

His gut clenched. Escort *this woman?* He'd never be able to keep his hands off her. Honor and courage radiated from her, and he knew she was one of the few people in his life who he would have admired, if he'd ever had that luxury. "I would be honored to," he said quietly, speaking directly and only to her, "but I have another mission I must address. I can't assist you."

She looked up at him, and he could see the shadowy outline of her face in the faint blue glow from Rohan's sword. Her cheekbones were high and regal, and her hair appeared to be dark. Her lashes were long and thick, but he couldn't discern her eyes. He *needed* to see her eyes.

"I'll make it worth your while," she said, a hint of authority in her voice. "I can assist you with whatever your mission is. I have a great many resources available to me, and they'll all be yours once I am safely at my destination."

Her voice was cool and reserved, but there was a desperation in her voice that she couldn't quite mask. She was in trouble. Big trouble. His protective instincts arose fast and hard. He narrowed his eyes. "What's going on? Tell me." Before she could answer, he felt a sudden cold draft. He looked up sharply, breathing in a scent of such evil that he went into high alert. "Danger approaches," he said softly. "There's something out there."

Rohan and Thano immediately called out their weapons with a crack and a flash of black light. Instantly both Calydons were armed with the weapons that Levi knew were etched on their forearms, just like his. Levi's weapons burned in his arms, but he couldn't call them out as long as the chains still bound him.

"That's what's after me," Maya said. "Please. We don't have much time." She reached up and put her hand on his ankle. *Please.*

The moment she touched him, electricity exploded

through him. Power and sex, and a burning so intense that he knew he couldn't rest until he claimed her. Her voice was like a sensual caress across his mind, for him, and only for him. He knew in that instant that she wasn't a psychic temptress. She was his. Forever. She was his *sheva*, the woman he was destined to bond with, the only person alive who would have the ability to touch his soul, the only one who would have the ability to kill the assassin no one could destroy.

And in that moment, he knew she was his answer. Once he killed his former master, he would be under the thrall of the bloodlust, and no one would be able to stop him...except his *sheva*, who was destined to kill him once their bond was complete.

The chill grew stronger, and he knew they had only moments. Maya had suddenly gone from a temptation to his only chance of success. "I'll do it." He would help her, complete the *sheva* bond with her, and make her kill him after he destroyed his former master. It was perfect.

He felt her relief instantly, and in that moment, for a split second, he didn't care if she was going to aid him. All that mattered was that *he* had made her feel better, that *he* was going to protect her.

"Let's do it." Blue light glowed from Rohan's sword, and Levi swore, turning his head into his arm again to shield his eyes.

And then, he heard the sound of metal against metal, and suddenly, the tension on his arms and shoulders were gone. For a split second, he was weightless, and then he crashed to the floor of the cavern, his legs giving out the moment he landed.

For a moment, he couldn't move. His body felt like it didn't belong to him. His arms were numb, and his legs were twisted beneath him.

"Let's go." Rohan slashed again, and suddenly, mercifully, the chains fell away from his arms. He was free.

Chapter 2

Maya was shocked when Levi crumbled to the earth, collapsing onto the hard ground as if his body was made of jelly. The muscles in his legs were toned and defined, but when his feet hit the ground, they appeared to simply give way under the weight of his body.

"Levi!" She instinctively lunged forward, her hands outstretched to catch him, but Rohan grabbed her and hauled her back, letting Levi crash to the ground.

She flinched at the sound of his body slamming into the stone floor, as if all his bones had shattered upon impact. He didn't move after he landed. He simply lay there on his back, one arm flung across his eyes to shield them, his chest heaving as he sucked in air, as if they were the first deep breaths he'd taken in decades. The chains were still wrapped ruthlessly around his arms, and she could see they were some kind of black metal, crusted after all the years below earth.

Rohan swung again. His blade sliced cleanly through the chains with a faint whisper, and the chains clattered to the rock. Levi groaned and pulled his arms to his chest, cradling them against his body, his eyes squeezed shut. The glow from Rohan's sword flared brightly as he struck, giving Maya her first clear view of Levi. Her stomach roiled when she saw that the skin on his arms and hands was charred and blackened, as if the chains had killed the flesh it had bound so tightly.

His body was ripped with muscle, but he was lean, so incredibly lean. She could see his ribs with each breath, and his hipbones jutted out beneath his pants. He was wearing only pants. No shirt, no shoes, no socks. Half-naked and chained up for over a century. How was he still alive, let alone sane? Her heart constricted for his suffering, and she wanted to kneel beside him and offer comfort that she knew would change nothing, but Rohan's grip was still tight around her wrist, relentless even when she tried to twist free. "Let me go."

His voice was low and rough. Unyielding. "Not until we're sure he's safe."

"He *is* safe!"

But Rohan's grip tightened. There was no way she could break free, even though he was being careful not to hurt her. Frustrated, she glared at him, but she couldn't see his face beneath the hood of his cloak, and she had no idea if he was even looking at her. She gave up, and turned her attention to the man on the ground. "Levi! Are you all right?"

Levi took another deep breath, and as she watched, she could see the strength returning to his body. His muscles rippled, and his breathing became more even and steady, less labored. The brands on his forearms appeared to be an ancient double-sided Lochaber axe. One blade was a fierce point, and the other was a curved half-circle that reminded her of a crescent moon, glittering in the darkest of nights. The handle was even more dangerous, loaded with a razor-sharp spear point, which was flanked with two deadly blades that mirrored the larger ones on the other end. The weapon was a fierce, deadly implement from all angles, and she shivered at the idea of what kind of damage he could inflict with it.

Even lying inert on the ground, Levi gave off an aura of such strength and power that she had no doubt he was every bit the legend Rohan had claimed he was. He raised one blackened arm and flung it over his eyes. The moment he did so, she saw his body relax, as if the light from Rohan's sword had been hurting him.

"Get up," Rohan snapped, his fingers loosening around her wrist, as if Levi's lack of movement had reassured him of Levi's ability to restrain himself from going on a murder spree. "The wolves are closing in. You need to go."

Rohan's command jerked Maya into action. She twisted

her arm free, and this time, Rohan let her go. She raced over to Levi and knelt beside him. "Levi?" She leaned over him, not sure whether to touch him. "What can I do to help?"

"I'm all set. Thanks." His voice was soft, rolling over her like a soft caress that made her entire body warm. "Shut the light off, Rohan," he commanded in a completely different tone than the one he'd used for her. His face still buried in his upper arm, he shifted awkwardly onto his knees, swaying as he tried to find his equilibrium on the solid ground. "Now."

Rohan shook his head "We need it to fight the wolves," he said as he turned away from them to guard the tunnel. "Go!" Thano had whirled Apollo, his horse, around, and they were both facing the opening they'd just emerged from. The shadow wolves were following their path exactly. How had they found her so quickly?

God, she hoped Rohan was right about how good Levi was, or she would soon be dead.

"Here." She yanked off her coat, shivering in the frigid temperatures, as she started to wrap it around Levi's head. He stiffened, and suddenly, in a lightning fast move, he grabbed her wrist, yanked her over to him, and pinned her beneath him. His body was trembling, with cold or the effort, she didn't know, but his hands were holding her wrists above her head, with the kind of force a man would use against an enemy, not a seduction.

"Levi," she said urgently. She knew she should be afraid to be at the mercy of a deadly assassin, but she felt no fear. He was like a caged animal, striking out in self-defense, not aggression. So, instead of calling for Rohan or trying to fight, she soothed him. "It's me. I won't hurt you."

He didn't move for a split second, and she felt his energy warring within him, dark and light energy that refused to mix. He reached out with his mind, and she felt that same intimate touch brush inside her head as before. This time, she sensed the desperation within him, the need to connect, and she didn't block him. His energy seemed to wrap around her like a comforting, protective shield. She felt his body shudder with relief. Then, he swore and released her, rolling off her while he covered his eyes with his arm. "Sorry. Instinct."

"It's okay," she scrambled back to a sitting position. "I

was just trying to give you something to cover your eyes."

"Go!" Rohan shouted. "They're close."

Levi swore, grabbed the coat from her hand with unerring aim, then tried to tie it around his head. He fumbled and one of the sleeves fell from his fingers. She realized his fingers wouldn't bend, probably frozen after so long in the chains. "Let me." She sent him reassurance with her mind, and he dropped his hands at the same moment she reached for the sleeves of the coat.

He went utterly still, letting her tie it around his head. His hair brushed against her fingers. It was long and ragged, but incredibly soft. The dark strands drifted across the pads of her fingers, a temptation that seemed to call to something deep inside her. Heat rose in her cheeks, and she quickly tied the sleeves and pulled away. "All set."

The moment the blindfold was secure, he was on his feet, his hand tucked under her elbow to drag her to her feet. "This way." Even though he clearly couldn't see anything, he didn't hesitate as he pushed her toward one of the tunnels. "Fast."

She started to run, then heard him stumble. She whirled around and saw him swaying to the side, as if he were struggling with his balance. "Hang on," she said, as she raced back over to him. She slung his arm over her shoulder, and ran with him to the tunnel opening. He didn't resist, leaning on her as they went.

They sprinted through the opening. Then, suddenly, the ground gave way beneath her feet. She had no time to scream before they were free falling into a pit of pure darkness.

☒ ☒ ☒

Once they were airborne, it was simple for Levi to regain his balance. He'd been living in the air for a century, and it was the world he was accustomed to now. Free-falling was a hell of a lot easier than standing on the ground. He felt in control, and confidence surged through him. As they plummeted downward, he pulled Maya against him, locking her against his body. "Hold onto me," he instructed.

She immediately wound her arms around his neck, and he helped her lock her legs around his hips. Heat from her body poured into his, giving him strength and energy he hadn't felt in decades. The intimate position sent raw lust straight to his loins, and for a second, he could think of nothing but the feel of her body against his. It had been so fucking long since he'd had physical contact with another human being, and having Maya wrapped around him was incredible. Beyond incredible. It felt like she'd shaken his world to the core, and all he wanted to do was slide his hands down her hips and over her butt, drawing her even closer into him until there was no space between their bodies, until there was nothing left to do but drown in the sensation of her kiss and her touch—

"Um, Levi?" Her voice was edged with fear, but it was steady and calm. "What are we going to land on?"

Her question jerked him back to the present, and he swore at himself, unsettled by the fact that he'd lost his focus in such a critical situation. "Hopefully water."

Her arms tightened around him. "Hopefully?" The edge to her voice increased. "What's the other option?"

"That we'll be crushed against a wall of ice, but I think we'll be good." He locked one arm around her waist, using his arm strength to hold her there, since his hand still wasn't functioning that well. Even as he thought it, however, his fingers began to ache. He tried to bend them, and he got a tiny bit of movement. Healing already.

Oh, God. You're impossible.

He grinned as he held out his free arm, and felt the brand burning in his flesh, as it had so many times in the last century. This time, however, he could call it out. Intense rightness surged through him, and he smiled as he summoned his weapon. There was a crack and a flash of black light that bled all the way through his blindfold, and then he felt the steel of his ancient battle axe in his hand. Jesus. It had been so long since he'd held it, he felt his entire body hum in response as he once again claimed his heritage. Despite their stiffness, his fingers closed instinctively around the handle, merging with the weapon that was a part of him.

He immediately hurled it straight downward at the solid wall of ice they were speeding toward. The axe hit the ice cleanly, shattering a large section a split second before they crashed through the bobbing ice fragments into the frigid water below. *So, water, then.*

The ice water sucked the breath out of him. Maya's body constricted in shock, and he heard her gasp of pain in his mind.

It's okay, Maya. It's just for a few seconds. Take my heat. He pulled Maya closer, sending his own body heat into her as he kicked them to the surface. Their heads burst free as the river hurtled them away from his living grave. He called his weapon back, and it returned to the brand on his forearm as they were tossed ruthlessly along.

You're insane. You're not going to keep me alive. You're going to kill me. Maya gripped him more securely and coughed.

I would never kill you. Ever. He couldn't keep the fury out of his voice. He never used to care what people thought of him, but hearing Maya say it made him want to defend himself. He didn't even know her. He knew that. But it still mattered what she thought. He hoisted her higher against his chest, holding her head far enough above the water so that she didn't get splashed. *I'm not dangerous to you, I swear it.*

I didn't mean it like that. Maya's voice was gentle in his mind, as if she'd understood what he'd been thinking. *I wouldn't have gone with you if I didn't trust you. I was just commenting on the fact that plummeting into a frigid river beneath a wall of ice isn't the usual way to save someone.*

Okay, then. Relief rushed through him, and he couldn't stop the dumbass grin on his face. She trusted him. He liked that. *Hold on. It's going to get rough.*

Of course it will. I definitely felt like this was too easy. Her dry sense of humor made his grin widen, even as she tightened her grip on him.

Holding her tightly, he reached out with his psychic energy, assessing the landscape ahead, just as he'd done so many times from his prison. The river was turning, diverted by the pulsing geyser up ahead. He was just about to redirect them toward the geyser, when a thought struck him. *How mortal are you?* The geyser could incinerate her if she were mortal.

I'm about a nine on a scale of twelve. Why? Because that's not really the kind of question that's reassuring, you know.

Nine on a scale of twelve? Who has that kind of scale? He swore under his breath, quickly searching ahead for an alternate exit, but the river was heading deeper beneath ground. He could feel Maya trembling against him, and he knew they had to get out of the cold water soon. She'd be dead if they didn't. *Maya. If we take the exit, it could be a little tricky. I can heal you when we get out, but you have to trust me.* The only way he could heal her was if she was his *sheva,* and he was certain she was, certain enough to make this choice.

Her fingers dug into his shoulders. *Is there any other way?*

No. He couldn't keep the fierceness out of his voice. *I can protect you, but you're going to have to trust me. I mean, really trust me. You need to let me connect with you all the way.*

Oh, man. Personal intimacy stresses me out, but okay.

He grinned at her comment. *Trust me, I struggle with it a lot more than you do. We can fight the intimacy together, while we're hurtling toward each other on a psychic level. Sound good?*

She laughed, a light sound that seemed to lift layers of darkness from his mind. *Perfect. Okay, give me a sec.* He felt her summon sudden, intense strength. From deep within her came a source of energy unlike anything he'd ever felt. It was a distinctly female energy, filled with some sort of golden glow that he could almost see in his mind. It was pure strength, unfettered with all the sins that littered his soul. It was beautiful, and he was honored she'd let him experience it. *Okay, I'm ready.*

He tightened his arms around her, all his energy centered on her. *Let me in.* He touched her mind, and for a moment, he felt her resistance, and then she lowered her mental shields, opening herself to him on every level of her soul.

⊠ ⊠ ⊠

The moment Maya opened herself to Levi, he swept inside her mind, filling her with the raw power of his being. His strength was pure male, a cauldron of sex, danger, and intimacy.

He enfolded her in his presence, sending his energy through every cell of her body. His invasion was instantaneous and all-encompassing, sweeping through her so deeply she felt as if she had no secrets left from him. She started to panic. *Levi—*

I swear on my life I will keep you safe. The moment he spoke, she felt the intensity of his protectiveness, the depth of his commitment to safeguard her, and she knew he spoke the truth.

She was safe with him, truly safe, at least in this moment. *Okay.*

Good. He twisted his body, and she lifted her head from his neck just in time to see him call out his weapon again with a crack and a flash of black light. In one effortless move, he hurled it straight ahead. He didn't release the weapon, however, and they were jerked forward by the sheer force of the weapon's trajectory.

It dragged them out of the river, and she gaped as the river careened to the right, disappearing into what looked like a solid wall of rock that would have crushed them if they'd hit it. She turned around in Levi's arms to see where they were going. Ahead of them was a thick wall of steam, almost twenty feet wide, making the air so hot she could barely breathe. She knew that's why there had been no ice wall above them when Levi had dragged them out of the river. Unfortunately, she was as susceptible to boiling hot steam as a wall of ice would be: instant melt. *Are you serious, Levi? That will incinerate me.*

No chance. Levi's energy cascaded through her, coating her cells, encircling her body. *Tuck yourself against me as close as you can,* he commanded.

I really hope you're right. It was too late to back out. She immediately pulled her arms and legs inward, relying on him to hold her as she made herself a tiny ball in his arms, burying her face against his chest. He wrapped her up tightly in his arms, using his body as a human shield to protect her. He shifted their position so he was beneath her, and she knew he was going to take the brunt of the steam on his own back once they reached the geyser. *Isn't it going to burn you?*

Sweetheart, I've been dreaming of this race to freedom for a hundred years. I'm going to relish every last second of pain this thing gives me.

She had one moment of stunned surprise at the endearment, a moment where her heart seemed to turn over, and then they were in the geyser, being hurtled upward so violently she lost all sense of equilibrium and balance. For a split second, the heat assaulted her so viciously, she screamed in pain, and then Levi's energy filled her, protecting her, somehow shielding her from the worst of the heat.

She tucked herself more tightly against him as he held her, keeping them balanced as they were hurtled upward. The steam swirled around them, a violent energy trying to attack them both. Instinctively, she reached out to Levi with her mind, and his energy swirled through her. She felt his strength and his protectiveness, but she also felt a regret so great that it seemed to eat right though her heart. She felt the depths of his self-loathing, and the weight of a thousand destroyed souls weighing on his. She realized that despite his strength, he was more broken than anyone she'd ever met.

Tears were falling on her cheeks when they burst from the earth, and it wasn't from the pain of her own burned skin. It was for the decimation of his soul.

Chapter 3

As he and Maya were ejected from the geyser and spun into the air, Levi adjusted their trajectory to keep Maya shielded in his arms. No light tried to blind him, and he ripped off his blindfold. It was blessedly nighttime, and the darkness was his friend. Easily able to see in the semi-darkness, he quickly scanned the earth and then targeted a small pond as their landing zone.

Using his weight, Levi angled their descent, sending them hurtling toward the pool of water. *Hold your breath,* he commanded. Maya immediately inhaled, and he tucked her up against him, protecting her as they cannonballed into the water.

They hit with a tremendous impact and shot toward the bottom of the pool. He saw the ground coming up fast, and he immediately began kicking. He slowed them just before they slammed into the bottom, but the impact almost jarred Maya out of his arms. Stunned by the impact to his legs, he could barely move for a second, and then Maya grabbed his arm. *Come on!*

He somehow got his legs moving, and they swam up toward the top. By the time he reached the surface, his lungs were burning, even though there had been a time when he could stay under water for several hours at a time. He shot his head above the water, and sucked in air...fresh air. Air that tasted of grass, and trees, and sunshine. "Holy shit." He was out, really out of that cave. He could feel the difference in his lungs, in the way the air felt as it filled him.

"Come on." Maya swam toward the edge of the pool,

and he broke out after her. His body slid through the water the same as it had through the air, but it was different feeling the water slide over his skin. For so long, there had been nothing but still, invisible air touching him, and now, the warm water caressed his flesh.

He reached the edge of the pool and hoisted himself over the edge after Maya. His hands cramped when he braced them on the ground, but Maya grabbed his shoulder before he lost his balance.

He barely managed to drag his feet out of the water before he collapsed on the earth. His skin hurt from the contact with the hard ground, and his legs ached from hitting the bottom of the pond so hard, but it was the best pain he'd ever experienced. It was the pain of being free, of feeling his body do the things it was meant to do.

He rolled onto his back, staring up at the sky. The black night stretched endlessly, an eternity of freedom and space. He breathed deeply, feeling his lungs expand as he drank in the clean, fresh air, as he surveyed the expansive heavens. A crescent moon shone down upon him. Stars glittered and winked, as if they were alive. "Stars," he said softly. "I forgot about the stars."

Maya sat down next to him, not touching, but close enough that he could feel her soft, reassuring presence against him. "How long were you in there?" she asked.

"A century. Maybe two. I don't know exactly anymore." He didn't want to move. Before his incarceration, he'd never paused for even a split second. He'd always been on the move, never still, but right now, in this moment, he wanted to do nothing but breathe in the sense of freedom. At the same time, he wanted to get up and run, just to feel his body working the way it used to, to prove that there were no more boundaries holding him back. Run and stay. Move and breathe. A thousand different emotions surged through him, a thousand different urges, and yet he didn't move. He simply lay there, feeling the earth beneath his body.

Maya leaned over him. "Are you okay?"

He looked at her, and, for the first time, he could see her clearly. His heart slowed nearly to a stop, and the stars vanished, obscured by the sheer force of her being. The crescent moon cast enough light for him to see every detail of her face. Her hair was a deep auburn, utterly straight as it hung over her shoulders, almost touching his chest. Her eyes were a radiant blue, framed by dark eyelashes. Her skin was a vibrant almond color, and her lips were parted. But it was her eyes that riveted him. Not just the color. The determination, the fear, and the desperation. She was battle-tough, and yet terrified at the same time. So much emotion, so much depth, so much humanity.

Stunned, he reached up and brushed his fingers over her cheek, needing to touch her, to see if she was real. Her skin was feather-soft, unlike anything he could recall ever touching. "Like silk," he whispered. "Extraordinary."

Her cheeks flushed, but she didn't pull away. "Was it horrible?" she asked softly. "Being trapped like that?"

In her eyes, he saw an understanding that went far deeper than it should have. Instead of answering, he slid his fingers along her jaw. "Why do you know what it's like?" he asked. "What happened to you?"

She managed a small smile and shook her head. "Nothing like what you endured." But there was an edge of pain in her voice that told him more than she wanted him to know.

He narrowed his eyes. "You're hurt."

"No, I'm fine. I—"

"Come here." He reached up and grabbed her shoulders, pulling her down on top of him. She didn't resist, and her body was warm and flush against his. For a moment, the feel of her body against his shocked him, and desire rocked through him, the kind of sharp-edged lust that could consume a man for centuries and never let him go. Swearing under his breath, he forced himself to concentrate on the situation at hand. "My body is shot, and you're hurt. We need healing," he said. "I'm going to heal us both, but you need to let me in."

Her eyebrows shot up. "Like in the geyser?"

"Yeah, only more." Healing required a whole other level of connection, the kind that existed between Calydons, or between a Calydon and his mate. There was only one way to heal her, and she had to buy into it. He paused for a moment, debating whether to tell her the truth. The hesitation lasted only for a brief moment. They had no time to hide from the truth.

"Do you know what a *sheva* is?"

From the way her eyes widened in shock, he knew her answer was yes.

And she didn't look happy about it.

⚔ ⚔ ⚔

Maya felt as if the foundation had just dropped out of her world at Levi's question. "*Sheva?*"

At his nod, shock ripped through her. Suddenly, she understood the depth of her response to him, her absolute trust, and the fact that she could feel his emotions so deeply...and yes...it also explained her absolute awareness of him as a man when she had *no* time for men. She was his *sheva?* It all made sense, but heaven help her, that was not what she could afford right now. She tried to push off him, but his arms were too tight around her, keeping her sprawled across his chest in a position that no longer felt as comforting and safe as it had moments before. All the burns on her skin began to throb, and she had to bite back tears at the pain. "Let me up."

"No. We need to talk." It was so dark outside she could barely make out his features, but she could feel the weight of his gaze burning into her. "You know what a *sheva* is?"

"Levi, let me go!"

His arms softened, and she scrambled off him, trying to reclaim her space. "Of course I do. Who doesn't?" She walked several yards away, then turned to face him, her fists bunched at her sides. Her heart was thundering, and she was shivering from the trip through the water. "A *sheva* is the Calydon's soulmate. She's destined to bond with him, and once the bond is complete, he will lose her, turn into an insane killer, and destroy everything that matters to them. Once he goes rogue, the only way he can be stopped, aside from a flat-out assault by the Order of the Blade, is for her to kill him, and then she's destined to kill herself because she's so upset he's dead." Oh, God, seriously? That was just the worst fate ever. "So, yes, I know what a *sheva* is. Why are you asking me?" Oh, she had a bad feeling she knew exactly why he was asking, but maybe she was wrong. Maybe he wasn't going to make some dire pronouncement that their souls were inextricably intertwined, hurtling them toward certain doom that would eviscerate them both. She rubbed her arm and winced at the pain. She knew blisters were starting to form on her skin.

He propped himself up on his elbow. "You feel it too." His voice was low and husky, sending shivers along her spine.

"Stop. I feel nothing except I'm freezing cold from the water, and my skin is burned from the steam." When he opened his mouth to argue, she held up her hand, as if that would hold him off. "If you're going to bring up the sizzling connection between us, or mention the way your touch makes chills race through my entire body, you just give up. That's nothing more than basic Calydon lust. You know how you guys are, all hot and bothered, and I'm the first female you've encountered in a long time. That's it." The words sounded so good, but even as she said them, she didn't quite believe them. For heaven's sake, he'd been able to talk with her psychically. It wasn't like that was a talent she normally had when she met a hot guy. It didn't help that her skin felt like fire was eating away at her flesh either.

To her irritation, he grinned, his teeth glistening in the moonlight. "No woman has gotten me hot and bothered before. You're the first. I'm very disciplined. So, it's not that."

"Oh, God, of course you would be the one Calydon who would be all disciplined about sex." She shook her head, running her hands through her hair as she paced restlessly. Her body hurt in a thousand places from their recent escape, but she didn't care. She couldn't stand still. There had to be another explanation. "Listen, it's just lust because you've been chained up for so long, and because I've been, well, a little stressed. We're strung out, so we're drawn to each other as a respite from what we've been enduring. Besides, I'm already committed elsewhere, thanks so much, and there's no space for some fate-driven love affair that will destroy us both—"

He sat up so fast that she didn't even see him move. "There's another man?"

Her heart stuttered at the anguish and fury in his voice, and she sank to her knees, her legs no longer able to support her. "Oh, God, how can you care? You don't even know me."

He rolled to his knees, and knelt before her, cupping his hand around the back of her neck. His touch sent chills cascading down her spine, and she had to fight not to lean into him. "Are you involved with another man?" His voice was like ice, striated with a deep anguish that made her resistance fade.

"No," she said softly. "I'm not involved with another man. I'm not dating anyone or sleeping with anyone. I just made a bargain to save my kingdom, and part of that bargain is me."

His fingers tightened on her, and a muscle ticked in his jaw. "You don't get to deliver yourself to another man. I can't take it."

"You can't take it?" She sighed in frustration, his words increasing her tension. She knew of only one reason why he would react so strongly and possessively to a woman he barely knew, and she didn't want it to be that reason. "You don't even know me, Levi. You can't care that much."

"I do know you," he said, his fingers softening into a sensual massage on the back of her neck. "I know you're brave enough to hire two dangerous Calydons to help you find me. I know you've got the courage to go deep beneath the earth and track down a man known only for the swiftness of his assassinations. I feel the desperation that's driving you to make these choices, and I sense the fear that haunts you, that you refuse to bow to either of them. Yeah, I don't know what, specifically, your situation is, but I know *you*. My body and my soul have already claimed you, and I'll protect you from harm, no matter what, and you know it." His voice roughened. "And I can't let you give yourself to another man. It's impossible."

Her throat tightened at his declaration. She felt the absolute truth of his words, and it was shocking how good it felt to be claimed by him. She'd been battling solo for so long, and to have someone by her side just felt surreal. "You don't even know what I need," she whispered. "Don't make promises you can't keep, and you don't have the right to tell me what I can and can't do to save my kingdom."

He studied her. "Tell me what's going on. Tell me everything."

"Everything? Oh, God, it's so much." She took a deep breath, but the thought of what she was walking into was suddenly too much to take, on top of what she'd just been through with Levi. Despite her denial, she knew in her heart that he was right about the *sheva* bond. Dear God, how could they survive what was happening between them? The only possible choice was to split up, and hope that somehow, some way, distance could save them both...but just the thought of walking away from him made a sense of gaping loneliness swell within her, an emptiness even more all-consuming than when her parents were killed, leaving her and her sister alone when they were so young. She shivered, instinctively wrapping her arms around her torso to hold in what little body heat she still had. She was still cold, so cold, and her skin was burning from the trip up the geyser. A raging cold within, and a searing heat on the outside, all of it so intense she felt like she was going to be sick.

His eyes narrowed as he assessed her shrewdly. "Come on. Let me heal you first." He held out his hand to her. "Neither of us will get anywhere if we don't heal. The only way I can do it quickly is through the *sheva* bond. Don't let your fear trump your intelligence about what needs to be done. We need each other, and we both need to heal. We don't have enough time to do it naturally."

She looked down at his hand, and she knew it wasn't just a healing hand that he was offering her. It was the first step down a path that would destroy them both. But if she could save her kingdom first...well...that was her duty. If saving her kingdom meant accepting the *sheva* bond and all the torment it brought, then she had to face that fact. She knew she needed his help. That was why she'd come for him.

What was more important? Her own survival, or her kingdom's? There was no decision to be made. She had a duty to her people, and this sensual, lethal warrior was her only chance.

She supposed there were worse ways to die than by aligning herself with a man who was so incredibly sensual that his voice seemed to caress her every time he spoke. He was a deadly assassin who was willing to use every last bit of his considerable skills to protect her. So, yeah, it could be worse, right? This was a legitimate chance to save her kingdom and satisfy all her lifelong fantasies about a knight in shining armor sweeping in to serve and protect her, so that was good. There was only the slight drawback of either becoming a sex slave to a man she'd never met, or having to slay the warrior who was already winning her heart with his honor, his bravery, and his kindness.

"Okay. Let's do it." Slowly, still trembling from both cold and fear, she put her hand in his cramped and frozen fingers. He grinned and wrapped his fingers around hers, tugging lightly.

She let him pull her against him, taking a deep breath as she allowed him to enfold her against him. When she'd embarked on this journey, she'd been ready to sacrifice herself to make this happen, but dying a horrible death and having to kill her own soulmate was a completely different situation. Then again, gaining an ally like Levi was also different, and she wasn't going to deny that having Levi as her partner was an incredible gift, in a thousand ways. "I can't die until my kingdom is safe," she said. "I've made a promise. We can't complete the bonding until I've fulfilled my duty."

"Your duty." Irritation flickered on his face, it was gone before she could react, replaced with a thoughtful expression that told her that he had no intention of letting her sacrifice herself. She braced herself for his argument, but he didn't bring it up. "I won't let you die," he said simply, referring to the *sheva* bond, not the fact she'd bound herself to another man in return for her kingdom's safety.

She sighed. "I appreciate the sentiment, but let's not lie to ourselves. Fate decrees that's our ending—"

"We'll figure it out." He grasped her hips and pulled her against him. "Come here. You need me."

Heat and desire rushed through her at the feel of his body against hers, and she bit her lip. God, how much did she want to bury herself against him? The urge to wrap her arms around him and claim him as hers was so strong she could barely keep from doing it. "I don't like needing anyone." But she didn't fight him as he lowered them both to the ground. He stretched out on his back and tucked her up against him, nestling her into the shield of his body.

She sighed again, this time with a sense of peace and satisfaction she simply couldn't deny. His body was lean and muscled, and it just felt amazing to be encircled by his arms and pressed up against his side. The heat of his body seeped into her, deep in her belly where she was the coldest. He was like a great source of sensual power, wrapping around her, and making her want intimacy and a connection she didn't have time for. He was sheer muscle and strength, everything that she didn't have herself.

He wrapped his arms more securely around her. "Close your eyes."

She hesitated for a moment, afraid that if she really let go, she would have no more defenses against him. The temptation he presented was simply too strong. Maybe it was the *sheva* bond, or maybe it was simply him. Either way, his allure was mounting by the moment. "But it's not safe. We're being hunted."

He smoothed her hair back from her face, a touch so gentle and tender that tears sprang to her eyes. God, how long had it been since she'd felt safe and treasured? A lifetime, it seemed. How could she walk away from what he offered her, just because they were fated to some disastrous end? Who knew what would happen before they even got to that point? Maybe this was her last moment of peace and safety. Maybe he was her gift, that moment she'd been craving her whole life, and now, she had it, for this one instant.

"Sweetheart, I can hear, see, and smell every living creature around us for thirty miles. I'll know if danger is approaching. Close your eyes."

His voice was unyielding, his arms tight around her, and suddenly, she didn't want to resist anymore. She just wanted to stop fighting so hard to stand on her own, and she wanted to lean on him, and allow him to help her. Plus, her body was absolutely killing her from the heat.

Reluctantly, she let her eyes shut. The moment she did, she became even more aware of the feel of his body against hers. His legs were tangled with hers, his bare foot against the back of her calf. She could feel the slow and steady thud of his heart, and she could feel his ribs expand with each breath he took. Yes, he was the cold steel of a warrior, but he was also a man who had suffered, a man who breathed the same way she did. A man who, no matter how much she resisted, she was connected to.

He touched her mind, a strong warmth that eased deep into the furthest recesses of her soul. *Tell me why you're scared.*

She sighed and snuggled more deeply against him, her

body relaxing against his strength. *Bad guys are hunting me.*

He chuckled, his chest moving beneath her cheek. *I gathered that. Why are they hunting you?*

She yawned. *They want to suck the life from my kingdom.*

His energy began to move through her body, healing each cell as it went, like a magical white light chasing away the deepest cold from her. *You're the queen?*

Technically, but only because my parents are dead and my older sister is in a coma. If she can revive, it's hers. She thought of Elisabeth, slowly dying, and tears filled her eyes. *The shadow wolves hunt our kingdom every few decades, preying upon the souls of the powerful. They attacked when I was little, and killed my parents. My sister has been queen ever since, but they came again five years ago, and almost killed her. I've been trying to figure out a way to protect the kingdom ever since, but they're gathering on the horizon again, so I'm out of time. They're coming for me. I'm the only one in my family left, and once I'm dead, there's no one to protect our kingdom.* She thought of all the villagers standing on the hill to the south of her kingdom, watching the ever-darkening sky as the shadows gathered, and how they'd all looked at her to save them. *I need to secure the kingdom's safety before the shadows take me.*

What are the shadows? His voice was soft and soothing, lulling her to sleep.

A dark energy from another realm. It takes the form of wolves, but they aren't real wolves. I don't know exactly what it is. I tracked Rohan down because he's an expert at defeating dark creatures, but he said he can't stop them. He and his team are trying to keep the village safe until I can secure their safety. She yawned again, surprised by how relaxed she was when talking about the horrors she was facing. Somehow, being with Levi made her feel less vulnerable. He made her feel like she had a chance, which was funny, since he actually increased the odds of doom and disaster.

But it didn't feel that way. It felt like, as a team, they were stronger than the forces hunting them, whether it was the shadows or an ancient Calydon destiny. She took another deep breath, and her mind began to slip into the fuzzy state of sleep.

Are you making me go to sleep?

I'm helping you relax. Calydon healing power works best through sleep. It'll take only a few minutes. We're not too bad off. How are you going to save your kingdom?

I made a deal. Sunlight for the kingdom, he gets me as his... Concubine? Servant? Minion? *He gets my loyalty.*

Levi stiffened, but she was too tired to care. She hadn't slept well in so long, always desperately working on finding the solution to preserve her kingdom's safety before the next attack. She hadn't slept at all since the first sighting of the wolves several weeks ago. But in Levi's arms, she felt safe, safe enough to finally relax for a few minutes. He wouldn't let the shadows kill her, and Rohan's team was guarding her kingdom.

She had a moment, a brief, brief moment, to regroup, a short respite before she entered a hell from which she knew there would be no escape, a hell that had absolutely nothing to do with Levi.

What exactly is the deal? With who? Levi's question sounded distant, too far away to answer. Her mind was too tired, and she didn't want to think about what she'd promised to save her kingdom. Putting it into words would make it real, and she wasn't ready to do that. Not yet. Not now. So, instead, she simply sighed, and let him take her to sleep.

There would be time to fight the battle when she woke up.

Chapter 4

Maya would die.

It was the first thought Levi had when he awoke from his healing sleep, still wrapped tightly around Maya. If he completed all the steps of the *sheva* bond so she would be able to kill him, it would trigger the fate that would result in her death. *Shit.*

He knew that. He'd known it from the start, when he'd agreed to help her, but it was completely different now. Before, she'd been a stranger. Now that he knew her as a courageous woman who was willing to sacrifice herself to save others…the thought of her dying for him just didn't work anymore. But what other choice did he have? Allow a madman to live and victimize others? He couldn't do that. He couldn't live with any more deaths that he could prevent. But he also couldn't let her die.

Shit.

He ran his hand through her hair, letting the soft strands drift over his fingers…and he realized he could feel every detail of the touch. Sensation had returned to his fingers. Like silk, the softest spun threads, beyond what he'd ever felt. He lifted his hand and watched his fingers flex. They moved easily, fully healed again. He flexed his wrist, studying the way the bones and tendons slid beneath his skin, no longer crushed and broken from a century in shackles. His shoulders no longer ached, and it didn't hurt to breathe. Power seemed to hum through him, and he knew he was back at maximum capacity.

Was it simply the healing sleep, or was it something more? Was it because Maya ignited something with him, something that only she could touch? He suspected it was more than simply the healing sleep. How could it not be? She was his other half, bound to him on a metaphysical level that no one quite grasped, and now she was with him, merging her energy with his.

He wasn't going to deny it felt right as hell to have her in his arms, and to be feeling so alive that he could defeat any enemy, no matter what. He was back at full strength, the same as he was before he'd been chained up, but he was also totally different, mainly because he wasn't insane anymore...

But the moment he thought it, that insidious, ancient craving began to pulse through him. That need to feed upon a soul. That hunger that was never fully sated. The lethal instinct that had trapped him for so long. It was still there inside him, still hunting for prey.

"Shit!" How could it still be there? He set Maya aside and sat up, resting his forearms on his bent knees as he bowed his head, fighting to suppress it. But still it came, a ruthless compulsion to hunt and feed. It came hard and fast, as if it were trying to make up for a century of being dormant. It was that relentless need to kill that had made him such a ruthless assassin. After all that time in the cavern, the need had abated, bled away by the isolation.

He'd thought it was gone. It had merely been sleeping.

He leapt up and paced away from Maya, fisting his hands as he tried to focus. He'd suspected it would come back if he killed again, but he'd also thought that as long as he abstained, he'd be okay. He'd thought he was *safe*, at least for the moment.

"Levi?" Maya was right behind him, and he jumped, spinning around and putting distance between them. "What's wrong?" she asked.

He spread his hands, as if he could push her away. "You need to leave. Now. Distance yourself from me." Her hair was tousled from sleep, tumbling wildly around her shoulders. She looked sleepy, vulnerable, and sexy as hell and he wanted to drop to his knees before her and simply breathe in who she was. But instead, he walked away, turning his back on her as he moved several yards away.

"I can't leave. I need you." Her words were simple, straightforward, and unapologetic, making his gut twist.

He wanted to be that guy for her, the one who helped her when she had no one else to turn to, but not at the cost of her life. He gritted his teeth and kept his back toward her. "Don't you get it, Maya? I'm an assassin. The compulsion to hunt was trained into me, making it a part of my very soul. I *have* to kill. That's how he controlled me. He kept me locked up until the need became too strong, and then he'd give me a target. I was so crazed with the need to kill that I did it, every time. I never hesitated, and I never looked back. It was..." Shit. What a nightmare that life had been. "It was a constant cycle of insanity and death. I was a monster, and I didn't even care." Unable to resist, he turned slightly so he could see her face, needing to know if she judged him, even though he wanted her to be smart enough to see him for who he was.

She pushed her hair out of her face, frowning at him. "But you're not like that anymore."

"I thought I wasn't. But it's still there." Jesus. It was still there. "Without him to give me targets, I might hunt you." The thought chilled him to the bone. He'd never hurt an innocent, but he'd also always been given prey to target. What if he wasn't given an outlet? What would he do then? "I kill. It's what I do. It's what I have to do."

She walked up to him, unafraid, so boldly that both fear for her safety and admiration for her courage coursed through him, warring factions in a body already stained with so much violence that there was almost no space for anything else. "Levi." She put her hands on his chest, and the shock of her soft touch was a jolt to his system. "There are really nasty things hunting me. You'll need to kill them to keep me alive." She smiled. "You'll get your chance to do your hunting thing, so it's all good."

Something inside him seemed to ease at the feel of her touch, and despite his attempts to be heroic and keep her at a distance, he found himself putting his hands over hers, holding them in place. "If I kill anything," he said quietly, "I will lose what is left of my mind. It's like an addiction. It's a need that's always there, and once I have the smallest taste of it, I'm lost to it. It took me thirty years in that hellhole before I was sane again. I don't want to go there. I can't live like that again, but the need is there, clawing at me, every second." He needed her to understand what he was. "Maybe I should have stayed chained up. Maybe the man who locked me up was right that the cavern was the only safe place for me." The thought was grisly, but he couldn't lie to himself. The night that he'd been ambushed by pissed off commoners after he'd killed their leader, he'd been knocked out, taken underground, and deprived of the ability to hunt. For years he'd raged, until slowly, the need to kill had begun to fade, replaced by the first glimpses of sanity he'd had in a long time. Getting chained up had been his greatest gift, because it was that isolation that had given him his mind back.

Maybe he should have stayed there. Maybe he'd been wrong to escape. Maybe he'd been wrong all this time to think he could stay sane once he was out.

Maya studied his face, her beautiful, intelligent eyes searching his, her expression devoid of any fear or wariness. "How do you kill? With your weapons?" She touched his arm, her fingers brushing over the brands that had been locked down for so long.

He shook his head, but didn't move away from her touch. It just felt so amazing to feel her skin brush against his. He'd been without human contact for so long. Maya's touch made him feel like he was a human being, like his soul still existed somewhere in the depths of all the stains he'd poured into it over the centuries. "Through the skin. I absorb the life force of my victim. Silent and unseen, I suck the life out of them until they're nothing more than an empty physical shell." He didn't try to sugarcoat it. As much as it would break him to walk away from her, he couldn't lie to her about who he was. She deserved the truth.

Her eyebrows shot up, and she pulled her hand back from him, breaking physical contact. "What about your Calydon weapons?"

He shrugged casually, even though a part of him shriveled and died at her retreat. For his entire life, he'd lived in isolation, and he was fine with it, but Maya made him burn for connection with her. To be so close, and then have her retreat actually made his chest hurt.

"I don't kill with my axes," he said, trying to stay focused on the conversation, and not on how badly he wanted to bury himself against her. "And I don't kill by accident. You can touch me without being afraid." He hadn't meant to say it, as if he were trying to convince her to touch him, but the words had come on their own. No one had touched him voluntarily in his life, at least that he could recall, except to hurt him. Even if people hadn't known who he was, they'd sensed how dangerous he was, and they'd stayed away. A few women had been attracted to the danger, but their touches had been clinical and meaningless, only for the purpose of getting a night of hard sex. Maya was different, and it made him want more.

She glanced at his arms again, but didn't touch him. "If you did use your weapons to kill someone, would it trigger the old cravings?"

He felt like his blood was on fire, burning through him with the need to touch her. Was it because she was his *sheva*? He didn't think it was. She represented more than a mate to claim. She was the life force he'd been searching for, the energy that could sustain him forever, the one that would fill him with all he'd ever wanted to be. He was hungry for her, hungry to the depths of his soul, not as predator and prey, but as if a part of his own soul had gone missing, and she was the key to making him whole again. "No, using my weapons is just a path to doing what I need to do, which is feed."

She cocked her head, studying him thoughtfully. "So, if you defended me with your weapons, it wouldn't trigger it? You could murder that man you want to kill with your weapons, and you'd be fine? Is that what you're saying?"

He stared at her, processing her question. Slowly, he realized that she somehow believed there could be an easy solution to this. "There's no happy way out, Maya. I was locked up because there's no way to kill me, and no way to stop me. You're the only one who can kill me, if we were to bond completely. Even if I don't use my powers to kill someone, I can tell the need is building again. Killing someone will make it happen faster, but it's going to happen. I need you to kill me before it takes over." There. The truth was out. The ugly fucking truth. It was completely foreign to be standing here, being honest with someone, but with Maya, he had no other choice. He needed her to know him, to see him for who he was, to give her the truth no matter how ugly.

She stared at him. "Really?"

"Yeah."

"That's why you said yes to helping me? Because you planned to cement the *sheva* bond with me, and then have me kill you?" To his surprise, she didn't look horrified. She looked *thoughtful*.

He nodded. "Yeah."

"Huh." She walked past him, stopping just beside him, but facing out toward the woods, as if she were thinking. Her shoulder was so close to his that he could feel the heat from her body. "And if I killed you, then I'd kill myself, right?"

He balled his hands into fists. "I already said that won't happen—"

She turned back toward him, and her eyes were bright with determination. "There is only one thing that can save my kingdom from the shadows, and that's light. They're natural opposites."

He narrowed his eyes, studying her, suspecting that she was about to propose an idea he wasn't going to like. Yeah, he admired her bravery, and he appreciated the fact she was working her ass off to save the kingdom, but there were limits to what he wanted to hear. "So?"

"So, there's a man who is the heir of an ancient kingdom of sunlight. He's the one I bartered with. His sunlight for my kingdom, and he gets…" Something flickered in her eyes. Fear? "He gets me."

Levi's gut hardened, and his fingers instinctively wrapped around her wrist. "What exactly is your deal with him? You said you weren't engaged."

"No, not engaged. Under agreement to help my kingdom." She grimaced. "I owe him fealty. Not as queen, as a woman. Not marriage, because that would be mutual. It's one-sided, me to him for my lifetime." She met his gaze, and he saw in them something he didn't like: fear, the kind of deep, knowing fear that would haunt a man forever. "He's a bad man, Levi. He'll hurt me. I know that, but it's the only way to save my people. I owe them that. But if you and I bond after my kingdom gets his light, and I kill myself afterwards." She managed a smile. "Then I'm free from him."

"No." He tightened his grip on her wrist, his mind spinning with the number of things he didn't like about that plan. "If he's a bastard, he'll hurt your villagers, too. You realize that, don't you?"

She met his gaze, lifting her chin like the royalty she was. "He doesn't get my kingdom. He just gets me. There's a difference."

"If he marries you, he becomes your king."

She shook her head. "Not in my kingdom. We're not getting married, and even if we were, you can't marry into the throne. You have to inherit it, or be declared."

"And if you die? Who inherits, or will be declared?"

She stared at him. "I don't know. There isn't a succession plan. I always thought…I never thought it would come to this. I wasn't…I wasn't planning to die when I started this. I was going to just endure, but…" She sighed, and her shoulders sagged. "Honestly, Levi," she whispered, her voice trembling. "I am not sure I can survive him. I'm scared. Really scared. Dying with you might be better."

Hell. What kind of future was she giving herself? Eternal torture at the hands of a bastard, or death? Both options made him want to drag her against him, call out his axe, and cut down anyone who tried to harm her. But he could already tell that she didn't want to be rescued, not if it meant letting down her people. So, he tried the only tactic that he knew would get to her. "What if he takes over your kingdom?"

She was silent for a moment, and he saw the reality in her eyes. "Without him, they will all die. With his sunlight, they have a chance. It's up to them to save themselves after this."

"He's so bad that you're willing to die instead of endure him, yet you'll leave your kingdom in his hands?"

"It's not in his hands! He doesn't get it!"

"He'll get it. You know he will, if he wants it."

She stared at him, and then frustration rolled across her face. "What do you want me to do, Levi? Let the life be sucked from their bodies until they're nothing but shriveled husks, rotting away? What kind of life is that—" Her face suddenly paled. "Oh, my God. Is that what you do? Are you like them? Are you...a shadow?" She backed away from him. "Are you what killed my parents? And my sister? Is that why you were able to sense them in the cavern? Is that what you are?"

Levi caught her wrist before she could retreat. "I don't know what's hunting you, but I'm the only one of my kind that I know of. I've never preyed upon an innocent."

"How do you know? Didn't you say you lose your mind?"

The fear in her eyes seemed to ice right through his veins, and into his heart. After a lifetime of not caring what anyone thought, his brief exposure to Maya had changed everything. She was the one person who'd ever seen him as someone other than a monster, and he couldn't lose it. As long as she saw him as worth trusting, he knew there was hope for him. Without that ray of hope she gave him, he had nothing to hang onto. "Don't," Levi said softly. "Don't do this to me."

Maya's eyes widened, and she stared at him.

For the longest moment, they simply stood there. Their only physical connection was his hand around her wrist. His grip was tight, but not so tight she couldn't break it, and they both knew it. And yet, she didn't pull away.

He felt like she was holding his world in her hands. His very soul hung precariously, awaiting her words, and his only chance at hope was in her control. He was teetering on the razor-thin edge of sanity, and he had no tools to defend against the dark needs humming away inside him. Maya was his light, the one thing that seemed to ignite his humanity. "I need you," he said, his voice roughened with emotion. "Despite everything I said earlier, I need you to believe in me."

Still, she didn't move, and he felt hope crumbling. The beast within him laughed, a bitter, satisfied laugh of triumph, and he felt the darkness swell within—

Her expression shifted into shock. "I feel that," she said. "I feel it inside you. It's...evil. It's like...death itself."

He shrugged. "It's not evil. It's just instinct. A need to kill." Even as he spoke, he heard that distant thundering sound, the one that felt like a thousand snare drums in the distance, getting closer with each second, even though it was inside his own head. Crap. It was the sound of the hunt amassing within him—

"No!" Maya suddenly flung herself at him.

He barely had time to grab her hips before her body smashed against him. The need for her was so great that he didn't even think as she flung her arms around his neck. He just hauled her up against him and kissed her. He poured himself into the kiss, drinking in every last bit of goodness and honor in her soul, his body literally shaking with desire as she kissed him back.

Her lips were soft and decadent, but her kiss was fierce, a weapon she was using to claim him back from the darkness within him. He realized she'd claimed him as one of those under her protection, just like her villagers.

Something tightened inside him, a realization that this petite, fiery woman who he could kill in one breath had declared herself his champion. He was one of the most deadly assassins in history, and yet he had a protector. Somehow, she'd seen his one weakness, the one war he couldn't fight himself, and she'd given him what he needed...which was her.

Chapter 5

Maya felt the moment that Levi succumbed to her kiss. His arms locked around her and he dragged her against him, until her breasts were crushed against his chest. His kiss was electric, plunging deep inside her, past all the walls she'd erected so long ago to protect herself and her heart.

She felt his pain. She felt centuries of guilt. She sensed the depth of the stains on his soul, and she could feel the intensity of his need to hunt, the power of the darkness within him. But inside him, buried deep, was something else. Humanity. Kindness. Empathy. A sense of self-worth. Things that were barely alive anymore, the things that she'd sensed in him that first moment when he'd touched her mind so desperately, as she was approaching him in the tunnel.

He deepened the kiss, his hands locked on her hips as he held her against him. She couldn't believe how good it felt to be kissing him, to feel his body against hers, to be so wound up in the sheer power of his kiss. He was dangerous, yes, of course she knew that. But at the same time, she felt his instinct to protect her. She'd seen it in his eyes when she'd told him her plans. She'd felt it in his kiss. And she could hear it in the tone of his voice when he'd said he needed her to believe in him.

For so long, she'd been in the role of the protector, for her dying sister and for her kingdom. It felt incredible to feel like she had someone at her back, at least for a moment. It was a completely different sensation from standing alone, fighting an enemy she knew was too strong for her, but knowing she had no choice but to see the battle through. Levi was powerful, insanely strong. He was a warrior who knew how to kill. It might be rather bloodthirsty of her, but she was in rather dire need of a man with those attributes right now.

His mouth was demanding and hard, and at the same time, his lips were soft, not bruising, as if he could somehow manage to keep all that hardness locked away behind his walls. His lips were a caress of pure seduction that stripped away every façade of independence that she'd erected so many years ago, making her entire soul yearn for connection with his.

She was desperate for more of him. Instinctively, she gripped the waistband of his pants. His stomach was rock hard beneath her touch, his muscles flexing as he deepened the kiss, dragging her tighter against his solid body.

She felt small and soft against him, but her body burned with need so hot that she could barely think. He was wearing only his pants, giving her access to so much skin. Her nipples strained against her bra, and heat pooled in her belly as the kiss ramped up.

Then, he slid his hands up her ribs. Her heart started to pound wildly in anticipation, but when his hands closed around her breasts, she was startled by the intensity of the sensation. Little shocks exploded through her body, and cravings wrapped around her. She wasn't even sure anymore if she were feeling her need for him, or his need for her, or some combination. All she knew is that she could feel every nuance of his emotions, the desire, the lust, the need to protect her, and the insatiable hunger for life…not death, life was what he craved.

I want this. His voice was rough and raw in her mind as he pulled her shirt and bra aside and caught her nipple in his mouth.

Oh, God. She gripped his bare shoulders, her legs shaking as he suckled on her nipple, sending fire rippling through every muscle in her body. *I do, too.* She knew she shouldn't want him. She knew she should stop. But she didn't want to. She'd spent a lifetime trying to prove to her parents and her older sister that she was worthy of the royalty she'd been born for. She'd worked so hard trying to be the woman no one thought she was, trying to play by the rules in hopes that she would finally be acknowledged as a worthwhile member of the royal family. After trying so hard to be *enough*, she didn't want to be the good girl anymore. She wanted nothing more than to surrender to the sheer magnitude of Levi's kisses, and the way he made her feel like no one else mattered to him, or ever would.

His soul was wrapped so inextricably with hers that she knew she was his breath and his light, the only thing that was sustaining him. He'd given her everything, even if he hadn't done it on purpose. His need for her was so great and so intense that it awoke in her all the protective and healing instincts that she'd showered upon her kingdom, but never on a person.

She wrapped her arms around his neck, pulling him closer for a kiss deeper than she'd ever offered, telling him without words that she was there for him, on every level.

God, Maya. There's no going back if we do this. Even as he kissed her, his hands were on the button of her jeans, his fingers flying through the motions as he unfastened them. *Making love is one of the bonding stages of the* sheva *bond. If we do it, we're on that path.*

She caught her breath as he slid her jeans over her hips and dragged them down her thighs. *There's no going back anyway, Levi. Not for me, and not for you. Bad things are going to happen for both of us, so why can't we take this moment, and live it? I want to breathe you into my soul and hold you there forever.* She knew if she bound him with the *sheva* bond, he would be hers forever, always there to help her. She would be safe with him, and she would have someone she could always, always count on. Until, of course, he went rogue and tried to destroy everything that mattered to either of them... there was that...

The thought made her stiffen. She'd forgotten about that aspect of the *sheva* destiny, that he was supposed to destroy everything that mattered to her...which was her village. Could she really manipulate the Calydon fate to serve her own purpose? Or would she be as much a victim to it as she was to the life she'd had as the second born daughter to a cursed kingdom? She didn't know. She didn't have answers. God, she was tired of not having answers!

"Maya." Her name was a reverent whisper that shivered

down her spine as he palmed her bare back, his hand nearly spanning across her entire lower back in a sensual reminder of exactly how much man he was. He kissed her again, stripping away all her thoughts and hesitations, until it was only him. *I want to make love to you.*

She pulled back, searching his face. "Will we lose if we do this? Will we?"

He paused, his hands on her hips. His eyes were dark and stormy, turbulent with emotions an assassin wasn't supposed to feel. "We might."

She swallowed. "But?"

"We might win, too." His fingers dug into her hips. "I won't force you, Maya, but if we don't want this, we have to walk away from each other. There's no way for us to be together and not bond. My need for you is too strong." He met her gaze, and she knew what else he wasn't saying. That his need for her to be able to kill him was equally as compelling.

Her heart seemed to break just a little "You want me to kill you? Really?"

He nodded.

"I can't do that—"

He caught her hands in his. "I need to die, Maya. It's just a matter of time until I become the assassin I once was. I am *not killable*, by anyone, ever, except you."

Tears filled her eyes. "I don't want to kill anyone."

"For your people? Would you kill for them?"

She stared at him, and nodded silently. She would do anything for the kingdom that was counting on her, the one that her family had never believed she was worthy of leading. She could do nothing else but give her all to her kingdom. It was part of her legacy, bound to her soul in a way that would never be denied.

Levi cupped her face, searching hers with his intense gaze. "I've never felt alive until I sensed you approaching me. I know my time is limited, and there's nothing I want more than to experience it through your eyes, through your emotions, and through the gift of what you give me. I want you, all of you. Your soul, your mind, and your body." He kissed her again, and his kiss was so pure and haunted that tears spilled forth and trickled silently down her cheeks.

She knew in that moment, that being with him was all she wanted. She knew what he meant when he spoke of a lifetime of an emotional desert. That had been her life too, stranded on the outskirts of a family who had no time for her, isolated and alone, even when surrounded by the people who were supposed to love her.

Being held by Levi was a gift she'd never experienced before, and she didn't want to miss out on it because she was afraid of what might happen in the future. He made her feel like she was worthy of being alive, plus he would be able to get her safely toward her goal. She needed him, on every level. And the future? It would be what it was. If she saved her kingdom, her life would be complete. She could ask for no more, other than to be with this man, this part of her soul, for this one brief moment to see what life could really be like when she was loved and treasured, and when she could do the same for another living being.

She entwined her hands behind his neck, and kissed him back, telling him without words. He growled low in his throat, and the kiss suddenly changed from poignant and emotional to a desperate need for possession. Excitement rushed through her as he took over the kiss, claiming her with each move.

He lifted her up, and easily removed the rest of her clothing in a single, effortless move before he wrapped her legs around his hips in an intimate pose that made her shiver with anticipation. His waist was lean and muscled between her thighs, sending chills of awareness through her body. Maya barely had time to process the intimacy of the position before he'd moved them to a bed of spongy moss. The vegetation was soft against her back as he laid her down, shedding his pants as he swallowed her up in his kisses and his strength.

The sensation of skin against skin was riveting, and she felt as if she'd been starved for his touch. She ran her hands over his arms and across his shoulders, wanting to touch every inch of him. He kissed his way down her body, whispering reverently as he went, the kind of intimacies that made her heart tighten with warmth. No one had ever made her feel like the world would stop spinning if she weren't a part of it, but in this moment, that was exactly how Levi made her feel. *Is this because of the bond? Is that why you affect me like this?*

He stopped kissing her belly then, and crawled back up her body. He braced his hands beside her head, his hips sinking low against her pelvis as his dark eyes searched hers. She felt his erection hard against her belly, but he didn't try to make love to her. He simply met her gaze, searching her face with ruthless intensity.

"The bond can make us want each other," he said. "But it can't make me appreciate your courage and your honor. I'm a master at feeling nothing, and yet you awaken every emotion inside me that I thought was long dead. I've stood over people I've killed, and never felt remorse. I've spent every night alone, and I've never felt isolated. I've never wanted a single moment of bonding with another person. But with you..."

He kissed her once, softly, his lips so gentle it was almost inconceivable that this brutal assassin was the one delivering such beautiful kisses. "But with you," he whispered against her mouth, "I feel like there's humanity within me. I feel my heart beat. I feel my soul stir. You make me feel alive, Maya, and that's simply you, because I'm too strong to be owned by the bond. I could stop what I feel for you, but I don't want to. I want to experience every single thing you give me, a thousand times over until there's nothing left in this world except how you make me feel."

Tears filled her eyes at his words. "That's very poetic for an assassin."

His eyes darkened. "That's how you see me, as an assassin?" He went still, and she felt his withdrawal.

She put her hands on either side of his face. "Of course I see you as an assassin. It's who you are. Do you really want me to lie to myself about who you are?" When his eyes narrowed, she laughed softly, and kissed his grim mouth. "But that doesn't mean that I don't also see that you're a good man. I see your honor, and I know that I did the right thing in tracking you down to help me. You're the only one I trust, Levi. You. No one else." She put her hand on his heart. "You need to know darkness in order to fight it, and there's so much darkness coming for me. I need you to keep me safe."

He still didn't move. "That's all this is to you? Keeping you safe? Is that why you want to make love? To cement the bond so you can die?"

She lifted her chin, refusing to acknowledge the sudden sense of loneliness that washed through her at his harsh tone. "I want you to make love to me because I want one good memory in my life before the bad ones start, and I can't think of anything that would sustain me more than being with you."

He searched her face, and she felt his presence in her mind, trying to ascertain the honesty of her words. She knew the moment he accepted her words as truth, and he kissed her again, a bruising, claiming kiss that said words he would never articulate.

She welcomed the kiss, opening herself to him as she felt his erection press against her damp entrance. For a split second, she hesitated. Was she really going to do this with him? Was he the one she'd been waiting for?

Yes, he was. She absolutely knew it. *Make love to me, Levi.*

Maya. His voice was a rush of desire in her mind, and then he sheathed himself inside her in one swift stroke, She gasped as he entered her, her body adjusting to his breadth as he went still, waiting for her to accommodate him.

Then he began to move, slowly, ever so slowly, each thrust sending tendrils of desire coiling through her. Desire twisted through her more and more fiercely, until it became an overload of sensation, of his body inside hers, of desire and lust and need and passion. All the sensations swirled around into a miasma of emotions that swept her up into the very essence of his being, until she could feel all his darkness and his pain bleeding into her, threatening to overwhelm her with its soulful song of mourning.

It's okay, Levi. I have you. She clung to him, and yet he held onto her even more tightly, holding her hips still as he drove into her, as a hundred years of captivity and torment spilled free from the prison he'd kept it in, swirling through her like a nightmare that would never end.

Levi. She grabbed his chin, dragging his face to hers so she could kiss him. His lips were cold, as if all the darkness had sucked the life out of him, but she didn't let go. She just kissed him with everything she had. He consumed her with his kiss, overwhelming her with sensation, thrusting deeper and deeper until the orgasm exploded through her.

She gasped his name, clinging to him as he bucked against her, dragged violently into her orgasm, eliciting a fierce climax from him, ripping through them until they were clinging to each other, hanging on to the one solid thing in a world that was spinning out of control. She could almost hear the whispers of fate laughing, and she shut them out, burying her face in Levi's neck as the final waves of the orgasm took her, until there was nothing left but them.

Exhausted, she sagged against Levi, her body aching from their lovemaking, a beautiful, amazing ache that somehow eased the emptiness that had been in her heart for as long as she could remember. He wrapped his arms around her and kissed the top of her head, his legs tangled with hers on their bed of moss, the scent of fresh earth and nature blanketing them like a fresh start.

Levi slid his hand down her arm and encircled her wrist with his fingers. He lifted her arm, turning his head to look at it. Even with the faint moonlight, it was dark, too dark for her to see what he was looking for. "What is it?"

He ran his fingers over her forearm. "The first stage of the bonding is done," he said, his deep voice comforting. "My brand will start to appear on your arm. With each stage, more of it appears. When we complete the final stage, the image of my weapon on your arm will be exactly like mine. Can you feel it?"

The moment he asked, she realized her forearms were burning, as if a hot brand was being etched across her skin. The brand was marking her as belonging to him. There was no going back now...and she realized, she didn't want to.

She was in until the end, whatever that might be.

Chapter 6

Levi watched silently as the silver lines appeared on Maya's forearm, as if an invisible pen were drawing them on her skin. The night was dark, but he still had the night vision he'd developed underground. The lethal, double-bladed handle of his axe appeared on her skin, an exact replica of the brand on his forearm.

An intense, primal satisfaction pulsed through him as he watched it. She was his now. He'd marked her, he'd claimed her, and he'd begun the process of sealing the bond. But even as some innate instinctive pride hammered through him, a dark foreboding pressed down upon him.

He knew all too well the fate of the *sheva* bond, her destiny to die by her own hand after killing him. His fingers tightened around her wrist, and he knew he could not let that happen.

He'd allowed himself to bond with her through sex only because he'd realized that there was one thing that would be more important to her than the death of her soulmate, and that would be the fate of her kingdom.

As much as destiny would try to get her to kill herself in despair after his death, he knew that she was stronger than that. She wouldn't die if her kingdom needed her alive, which meant that he had to find a way to make survival matter more to her than death.

He would die, but she wouldn't, and that was the way it would be. But as he brought her arm to his mouth to kiss the brand, something deep, deep inside of him rebelled at the idea of dying and leaving his woman alone to defend her kingdom without him. And what about the man who she'd bartered with? Would he really die and let her face him alone?

No. He wouldn't. The only option was to help her first, and then take her with him on his mission. And then…die he must, for the sake of the world.

She looked at him, those beautiful, courageous blue eyes fastened on him, drawing him out of his grim thoughts. "What are the other bonding stages? How many are there?"

He ran his hand down her arm, feeling the heat sizzling from her skin, focusing only on how good it felt to see his brand forming on her arm. "Trust is one of the stages. It's satisfied when we reveal our greatest secrets to each other, or give the other one the power to kill us."

She nodded, and bit her lip. "What else?"

"Death, where we kill to save the other one, or risk our lives to save the other."

She grimaced. "I can't kill anyone."

"Then we save that one until the end." He knew how the *sheva* bond worked. When the bond was tight enough, she would do anything to save him, and she wouldn't regret it, just as how she was willing to sacrifice herself for her kingdom.

Maya was a heroine, a protector of the highest sort, and he knew how she would respond when it was time. Until she was ready, however, he would not allow it to happen.

He took her fingers and played with them, marveling at how small her hands were compared to his. He knew they would have to get up and keep moving momentarily, but he wanted this moment with her. Lying in the moss with her entangled in his arms was the first normal moment he'd ever experienced that he could recall. It just felt…good. He didn't want to move. He wanted to be here. He wanted to experience this intimacy with her. He wanted nothing else for at least this moment. He wanted…peace, and in her arms, he felt like he could actually understand what it was. If he wasn't who he was, and if she weren't who she was, they would never have to move. They could lose themselves forever in each other, and in the moss that made their bed.

But that wasn't reality, and life had to move forward. "There's also the blood bond," he said, forcing him back to the conversation about the stages of the *sheva* bond.

She wrinkled her nose in distaste. "A vampire thing?"

"Kind of." He smiled. "It's a good one, actually." He'd heard other Calydons speak of the blood bond, a ritual that created a connection that lasted over all distances. He was glad he'd managed to escape Rohan without doing one, because the thought of being bound to anyone felt like a noose around his neck. But with Maya, it would be different. It would connect him to the feeling of being human that she gave him. "And then there's transference, when you can call my weapon into your hand in the same way that I can. It responds to you in the same way it obeys me."

"Really?" She flexed her hand, a small frown forming between her brows. "Show me how to do that. I want to learn."

He raised his brows, surprised by her response. "Most women would be trying to hold the bonding stages off, not encouraging them."

She looked at him. "Most women aren't being hunted by deadly shadow wolves who want to kill them, and most women aren't about to barter themselves to a man who wouldn't think twice about killing her if she didn't please him." She sat up, apparently oblivious to the sudden darkness that swirled through him at the idea of her coupling herself with another man. "I've been useless my whole life, Levi. A second-born princess trained to entertain other royalty and set tables, not defend her kingdom. If I'd known more, if my family had known more about self-defense, maybe we wouldn't be where we are. Will you train me, Levi? Will you teach me to be a warrior?"

Something shifted inside his chest at the eagerness on her face. Maya was petite, with a soft heart and a body that matched. There was nothing remotely fierce about her physically, but the fire in her soul seemed to ignite from within. That fact that she had no battle skills, but was still eager to learn, somehow made her seem all the more powerful and formidable.

He grinned, his respect for her growing even more. "Yeah. I'll teach you, on one condition."

She raised her brows. "And what's that?"

"You tell me everything there is to know about the shadow wolves preying upon your kingdom, and the man I'm supposed to deliver you to." He was not going to die with her bound to a bastard. He had to fix that first, no matter what.

She cocked her head, eyeing him with a bold perceptiveness. "There's no other option for me, Levi. You can twist the facts any way you want. I know. I've been doing it, and so did Rohan and Thano and the rest of their team. There's no other way. You can't save me from what I have to do."

He shrugged. "I've killed many people who weren't killable. Impossible means nothing to me. It's an illusion designed to weed out the weak from the strong."

Maya laughed softly. "What kind of argument is that? *'I've killed people who aren't killable, therefore nothing is impossible?'* I mean, seriously. That's the kind of logic people use to justify why stabbing a pitchfork through their own eye is a good idea."

Some of his tension eased at her laughter. "It's assassin life wisdom. Do you agree to the deal, or not? I turn you into a badass, and you tell me everything."

She sighed, and poked his chest lightly. "Yes, but I need you to take this seriously. The answer is not to find a new plan. My kingdom needs his sunlight, and there's no other way to get it. I've tried to negotiate with him for over two years, and I even sent a team to try to steal it, but they were all killed. This is the only solution, so I need to be able to defend myself. If you get your wish and I kill you, but manage not to kill myself, I'll need to be able to take care of myself, right?"

He wrapped his hand around her index finger, squeezing gently. "I don't like the idea of you having to defend yourself."

"Then come up with a solution besides you dying, so you can stay around and protect me."

"I can't. There's no other solution."

She raised her eyebrows at him. "Really? So, impossible means nothing when you don't agree with it? But when it's *your* conclusion, it's not changeable? What kind of life wisdom is that?"

He frowned. "It's different."

"It's not. On the chance I manage not to kill myself

after you die, or our plan somehow goes awry, then I need to be able to defend myself." She stood up, her body decadently naked in front of him. The moonlight cast her skin in tones of silver and gray, her curves accentuated by the shadows of the night. She was unashamed of her nakedness, and her boldness made him want to pin her to the ground and make love to her again.

But he'd made love to her once. He'd completed that stage. There was no need to do it again...except, of course, for the fact that he *wanted* to, which was unusual for him. He didn't crave women, and he didn't burn for physical intimacy. Or he hadn't, until he'd met Maya. He knew that as strong as the *sheva* bond was, it wasn't responsible for what was driving his need for her. It went deeper than that, and it was more than a simple, physical need. It was something primal, coming from the depths of his soul in response to who she was.

As if feeling his gaze upon her, she turned toward him. "Come on, assassin. Let's turn me into your best protégé before it's too late." She pointed toward the north, toward the highest peak in a distant mountain range. "I have to be there by sunrise tomorrow. We don't have much time."

Levi glanced absently at the mountain in question. "That gives me another night to make love to you—" His attention suddenly snapped to the mountains in the distance. A cold chill knifed through him when he saw the diamond shape of the tallest peak, raking through his bones like the assault of death. He knew that mountain. He knew it so well. That couldn't be the same one, could it? Could he really have been so close to it this entire time?

Sweat trickled down his temple, but he ignored it. "Maya," he said softly, his voice a lethal edge. "What is the name of the man you're planning to give yourself to?" He couldn't believe he hadn't asked that question before now. His life had been so insular, he hadn't even considered he might know the man she'd sold herself to.

She looked over at him, and her face paled at whatever she saw on his face. "Lord William Hotchkiss," she said. "Also known as Merk."

"Merk." He echoed the name that had haunted him for so long, and it bled through him like a dagger dragged across his bones. He dropped to his knees, staring out across the valley at the mountain in question. "You're going to sell yourself to *Merk.*"

Maya knelt in front of him. "What's wrong? You're scaring me."

He dragged his gaze off the mountain and grasped her shoulders, his hands shaking. "I was stolen from an orphanage when I was six, by a man who tortured me, twisted my mind and my powers, and turned me into an assassin." Memories flashed through his mind of his childhood, of the pain, the terror, the torment, but he shut them down, refusing to be weakened by them. "He created my compulsion to hunt and kill. He turned me into the monster I am. He controlled my mind, my soul, and my body, until all I cared about was serving him. I killed because of *him.*" He felt sick saying it, because it brought back all the hell he'd endured. It made it so real he could feel the acid burning through his flesh, and his intestines being carved out of his immortal body just to prove a point, and all the other things that had been done to him. "He's a monster, Maya. I was his pawn, but I wasn't the only one. There were other boys, boys who didn't survive the training. As long as he lives, there will be more like me, more boys who he tortures and turns into monsters, more people who get murdered because of his quest for power. He has to die, Maya, and I have to do it."

She nodded silently, her hands wrapped around his wrists. "Okay. I'm not going to judge you for that, if that's what you're asking. The guy sounds like he needs to die." Her forehead wrinkled. "You want to do that first? Is that what you're saying? Because—"

"No." He shook his head, his fingers digging into her shoulders. "His name was Merk, Maya."

Her face went sheet white, and she swayed. "What? I mean, I knew he wasn't a good man, but—"

"You can't do it. *You cannot do it.*"

She shook her head silently and held up her wrist. There was a black, braided bracelet around it made of steel, a bracelet he hadn't even noticed.

His gut turned to ice when he saw it, because he knew what it was.

Maya pointed to the bracelet, the magical noose that signified a metaphysical agreement that couldn't be broken. "The deal has been magically sealed. I'm bound to it, Levi. Unless I die first, I can't break my word." She met his gaze. "There's no way out."

"Then he dies." Levi surged to his feet, staring at the mountain, a hundred years of revenge bleeding through him like bile. "He dies first." It had been his plan all along, and now, it simply added fuel to his motives.

She didn't move from her knees. "If he dies, Levi, he takes his sunlight, and then my kingdom has no protection. He can't die, or my people and my kingdom are lost forever. He has to live."

Levi closed his eyes. "He has to die, Maya. *He has to.*"

She stood up, her hands fisted on her hips. "I won't let you destroy my kingdom, Levi. They're counting on me. I've never done anything admirable in my life, and this is my time. It's my duty. It's my heritage. *They must live.*"

He turned around to face her, and the brave, courageous face he'd admired so much was glaring at him with the absolute resolve to do whatever it took to save her kingdom, including stopping him from killing the man who had to be destroyed.

Chapter 7

Fear was haunting Maya. It was impossible to concentrate on her training when thoughts of Merk, Levi, and ghost wolves kept stalking her. Anxiety danced at the edges of Maya's mind as she tried to focus on Levi's weapon. *Come to me,* she ordered, using all her mental strength to command it.

Her hand remained empty, and his weapon stayed in his arm. "Dammit." She could feel the burning in her arms from the lines that were drawn there from the first stage of the bond, but no matter how hard she tried, she couldn't summon Levi's weapon. Frustrated, she set her hands on her hips, wiping the back of her hand across her forehead. "Why can't I do it?"

"Because there's no imminent danger." He was pacing around her, one axe called out and at the ready in his right hand. They'd been moving toward Merk's mountain all day, and he hadn't stopped watching it, or searching the woods behind them. "You can call it in times of need."

"Then attack me." She spread her hands. "Try to kill me."

He stared at her. "No."

"Come on, Levi! I need to practice with it!" She could barely keep her heart from pounding in terror, and she felt utterly defenseless after Levi's revelation. He hadn't said a single thing in response to her statement that Merk had to live to save her kingdom. Silence had fallen after her statement, his face had become a stoic mask, and then, he'd simply inclined his head toward the mountain and said they had to keep moving.

She knew what he was thinking. She *knew* he would try to kill Merk no matter what she said. His loyalty wasn't to her kingdom, so there was no way he could value it above his own motives of keeping her safe and killing the madman, which she understood, of course. But the kingdom was what mattered to her, and she knew she could never live with herself if she let him destroy the future of her people.

He would get her to Merk safely, but once they got there, their interests would diverge. Was that how it would end? Would she kill her soulmate to protect her kingdom? *Could she?* Her fingers shook at the idea of killing anyone, and Levi glanced over at her. "You're thinking too much," he said. "You need to have a quiet mind. Don't think about the reality of what you're doing. Just treat your opponent as a puzzle you have to solve before he figures you out. Let your mind whiz through the possibilities, learning his movements, his tells, and his weaknesses. Your mind must move at the speed of light, and you must allow your body to follow instinctively. You'll have no time for conscious thought."

He spun toward her, his axe aiming for her head, but not really, of course. She knew she could stand there and he'd never touch her. But since she was practicing, she pretended he was an evil killer. She ducked to the left and jammed her stick under his raised arm.

Levi raised his brows and stopped. "Really? You stuck a stick in my armpit?"

"Why not? Instinct will make you bring your arm down, won't it?"

He touched his neck. "Throat." He pointed to his crotch. "Balls." He tapped his rock hard stomach. "Abdomen, if you have a weapon. Those are my weak spots." He jammed his fingers toward his eyes. "And if I'm close enough, my eyes."

She dropped the stick, frustrated. "You defend those spots. I'll never get to them."

"Maya." He walked over to her and caught her arm, his eyes blazing. "Don't give up. You're better than you think. The armpit move wasn't bad. I'm just pushing you to get better." His fingers tightened. "Merk is a psychopath," he said softly. "He will hurt you every chance he gets. The moment you get close enough to his mountain that he can sense you, he will hunt you down and make you his in every way you don't want. You *must* be prepared to fight."

And just like that, the fear was back. "Stop it," she snapped, shoving away from him. "Stop trying to scare me into turning back or letting you kill him. Fear will make it impossible for me to function—"

"Hey." He dragged her against him, catching her in a bruising kiss. Instinctively, she softened against him, and she wrapped her arms around his neck, kissing him back. The moment she responded, his kiss gentled into a seduction that made her want to lose herself in him forever. *I'm sorry.* His voice drifted through her mind.

She pulled back to look at him. "You are?"

He sighed and brushed her hair back from her face. "Merk is the one man on this earth who scares me. I had no chance against him, and it took decades of isolation before I got my sanity back. I'm fucking terrified of what he will do to you, and yeah, I want you to get so scared that you run far away before he can get his claws into you." His arm tightened around her waist. "I swear I will do everything I can to keep you safe, but I don't know if it's enough. I don't know if I can defeat him. I couldn't before."

The fear in his eyes was real, and it settled deep inside her, mixing with the same fear that had been haunting her for so many years. "I've lived in fear since the shadow wolves attacked my kingdom and killed my parents. Every morning since then, when I get up, the first thing I do is look at the horizon and see if they're back." God, she'd never forget that daily fear, the aversion to opening the curtains and looking out. Her hands shaking every single morning that she grabbed the fabric and dragged it open, praying that they would be spared one more day. "Every night when I go to bed, I wonder if the morning is when they will come again. Three times, I've woken up and seen the shadows. The first time, they killed my parents and half the village. The second time, they attacked my sister, and more villagers. This time, it's me. I have to stop it. I *have* to."

Levi's face softened, and he sighed, his fingers sliding through her hair, carefully unknotting the tangles "I'm sorry, Maya. No one should have to live in that kind of fear."

She searched his face, and saw understanding beyond what she would have expected. "You know," she said softly. "You know about that fear." How did a lethal Calydon warrior truly understand fear?

He nodded. "When I was a kid, I was scared shitless, but I believed I could escape. I never truly thought he would win. Then I lost my mind, so I felt no fear when I was killing. I was too consumed by the madness. The real fear didn't set in until my sanity returned while I was hanging in that cave. I realized what I had done and how insane I'd been. The whole time I hung there, plotting my escape and Merk's murder, I knew he could find me at any moment. Every second, I waited for him to walk through those tunnels and find me. I was his best asset, and I knew he was searching for me. At any moment, he could have walked up to me, and I had no defenses. He would have reclaimed me, and I would have been lost again." He brushed the hair back from her face, his fingers tangling in the strands. "The moment Rohan cut me free, I felt the most intense sense of power. For the first time since Merk had kidnapped me from that orphanage, I had a chance to defend myself."

Her heart tightened. "So you understand why I need to save my kingdom from the shadows. I need to protect my people from the shadow wolves."

He studied her. "I understand why you need to save your kingdom, but there has to be another way."

She sighed and leaned her head against his chest, needing the feel of his strength around her. He wrapped his arms around her, enfolding her in the shield of his body. This man was her first line of defense and offense, but at the same time, he had the power to destroy everything for her. "I've been searching since my parents died," she said, unable to keep the weariness out of her voice. "I brought in so many experts, and no one knew what to do. Rohan is supposed to be a master of dealing with dark creatures. It took me forever to find him, but he eventually arrived at my kingdom with his team. He was there the morning the shadows arrived." She'd never forget that moment, when she'd opened her curtains and seen them. Her stomach had dropped, and a blanket of icy doom had descended upon her, freezing her into the immobility of true terror. "I couldn't believe it when I saw they were back," she said softly. "I wasn't ready, and they were coming for me."

Levi kissed the top of her head, listening to her words. He could imagine that moment when she'd seen the shadows, and the depth of her fear for her kingdom. He was impressed that she'd managed to recruit Rohan. The warrior was legendary in his battle skills, but also very elusive. He rarely, if ever, offered his skills to anyone. He had his own agenda, and never strayed. He wondered why Rohan had responded to her call for help. "What did Rohan say?"

She burrowed deeper against him, as if she were seeking protection from the memories, protection she hadn't been able to rely on when she'd faced it by herself. Levi tightened his arms around her, knowing they had to keep moving, but also understanding that they needed this moment.

"He said that they were creatures of darkness, predators made of smoke," she replied, her body fitting against his as if they had been created for each other, which, in a way, he supposed they had. "They take the form of wolves with red eyes when they attack, but they just dissolve under any blows. They don't stop until they are sated, and then they retreat. He said they usually defend ancient spirits, and it's unusual for them to be used offensively."

Levi narrowed his eyes as distant bits of memory floated past him. "I've heard of them. Rumors, only. I didn't realize they actually existed." He tried to remember what he knew of them, but so much from his past existence was a blur of blood-red memories.

She nodded. "Rohan said that, traditionally, they retreat when the danger to the ancient spirits has passed, but since they appear to be acting offensively in this case, they won't retreat." She ran her hands over his chest, as if drawing comfort from their connection. "Rohan agrees that sunlight would defeat them. When they come, they take over the sky and block out the sun. We need sunlight from within, so they can't block it. He doesn't know of any way to make it happen, though."

Levi considered this. "And you believe Merk has sunlight?"

"He does have it." She sighed, her face filled with grim

resignation. "He brought it once, long ago, to show my parents. He gave them a sphere that was lit from within as a wedding present. They kept it in their bedroom until my sister and I were born, and then they put it in the nursery. We were both in there with that sphere the first time the creatures came. They attacked the castle, and surrounded our room, but never entered. We could hear the screams as people were attacked, and we could see their red eyes racing past our door, and our windows. They snarled at us, and stalked around the room, but they never entered."

Levi felt the tension in her body, and knew the nightmares she must have had as a child. He'd had the same ones of Merk hunting him, because Merk had scouted him out before kidnapping him, stalking him at night and during the day, assessing his powers before selecting him. Merk had been the same as the wolves hunting her.

She ran her hands over his chest, moving restlessly, as if she were instinctively seeking comfort from his touch. He liked it, liked that her instinct was to ground herself in him when revisiting hellish memories. "After that night, my sister and I slept with the sphere every night. The next time they came, I was very sick with a fever. I was almost delirious. I heard them come, and I tried to get out of bed to find my sister, but I collapsed on the floor. I was lying there when I saw my sister running for the bedroom. The wolves were all around her, sucking her life force from her body. She lunged for the door, but fell before she could reach it. I—" Tears filled her eyes, and her voice choked. "It took me so long to drag myself across the floor, because I was so weak. I finally got her wrist and managed to pull her into the room. The minute she was inside the door, the wolves peeled away from her, howling in dismay, but it was too late. She didn't die, but to this day, she remains in a coma. I saved her, but too late." She searched his face. "I know what Merk has works, because it has saved me twice. I need enough to protect our entire village, forever. Don't you understand?"

Shit.

He did.

He got it.

But he didn't believe that allowing Merk to live was

their only choice.

Levi let out his breath. "I don't recall him having that kind of power source," he said slowly, trying to think back to what he knew of Lord William. "He must have acquired it, which means it could be acquired from him."

She stared at him, and for the first time, he saw hope in her eyes. "You don't think he creates the sunlight himself?"

"No, I don't. I would have known about it."

Her fingers tightened against his chest. "So...you think we could steal it from him? Or find out how he got it and then get some ourselves?"

"Yeah, maybe. It's possible."

"So, you can't kill him first, then. We have to find out about that power."

Levi ground his jaw. Every second Merk lived, he was a danger to both of them. If he'd targeted Maya, he wouldn't hesitate to claim her. Would Levi let him live long enough to hurt Maya? He looked down into Maya's blue eyes, and he knew the answer was no. If he had to make a choice, he would choose her over her kingdom. But if there was a way... "I think it's time to get some answers," he said quietly, intentionally not giving her the answer she wanted, that he wouldn't kill Merk until they had acquired their information.

She stared at him so long that he knew she'd realized his evasion. But to her credit, she didn't push it. "So, how do we do that?"

Levi looked up at the dark mountain. "I'm not sure yet." Merk was insane, but his security was impressive. At one time, Levi had known how to get through every safeguard, but he was sure they'd changed. "We'll assess as we get closer—" A sudden chill drifted across his flesh, and he spun around, calling out both weapons.

Maya paled. "They're here, aren't they? The shadows? They got past Rohan and Thano in the caverns?"

"Something is." Levi reached out with his mind, and he touched the rankest of evil. There was nothing about ancient protectors in what he felt. It was pure, predatory evil, and it was coming for Maya. Urgency coursing through him, he scanned the woods swiftly, searching for the wolves. They were coming fast, and he knew he couldn't outrun them.

He had to fight them, and from what Rohan said, his Calydon weapons weren't going to get the job done. He was going to have to go deep, to the places he didn't want to go. He spun around rapidly, trying to find a place to stash Maya. There was a small opening in a nearby rock, and he raced over to it. He crouched in front of the opening and reached out with his mind, assessing the interior the same way he'd inspected the tunnels around his prison while he'd been hung up there. It was small, empty, and enclosed. "There's only one entrance. Go in there." He pulled back and gestured to Maya. "Get in there."

She paused, looking at him. "What are you going to do?"

"Make me a promise," he said softly, as he handed her one of his axes. "If I cross the line and I don't come back, kill me. I won't live like I once did. Do you swear?"

She looked down at the axe in her hand. "You're going to kill them with your powers, aren't you?"

"It's all I can think of." He gripped her shoulders and dragged her against him. "There is only one way to kill me," he said urgently, searching her face. "Even as my *sheva*, you'll have to do it this way. Even if you do it, only the fact you're my *sheva* will make it work, because I won't be able to hurt you to defend myself." He jerked one side of his pants down, revealing a small, cross-shaped mark burned on the front of his hip, just below his pelvic bone. "You have to attack here," he said. "It's my weakest spot. You have to stab me there. Getting hit there can cause serious damage to me, but when fate helps you, I think you'll be able to kill me if you get me there. Got it?"

Her eyes widened. "Seriously? What are you? And how do you know that?"

The night grew colder, and he gripped her arms more tightly. He didn't have time to answer questions, or to think about the fact that he'd just given her information he'd never given anyone in his life. No one knew how to kill him, no one except Maya. "Do you understand?"

She nodded quickly. "I've got it." She grabbed his wrists. "But don't lose yourself! I need you!"

"I know you do." He kissed her once, hard, and then

broke away, shoving her into the crevice in the wall. As she crawled out of sight, as a deep sense of rightness settled over him. He knew he'd just completed his half of the trust stage by giving her the power to kill him. As he turned to face the night, he knew that there was another line being drawn on her arm, binding them closer together.

A low howl broke through the night, and he crouched, resting the fingertips of his right hand on the earth. The dirt was cold and wet, laced with rocks and the remains of the living creatures who had died there over the centuries. For a moment, he hesitated, his skin crawling at the idea of returning to that state that had once consumed him.

Then, directly across from him, he saw two glowing red eyes. As he watched, the shadows formed, taking the shape of a wolf. Two more sets of eyes appeared. The wolves spread out, encircling him on the three sides that were exposed, their upper lips curled in a deadly snarl.

He took a deep breath and calmed his mind, reaching out with his preternatural senses to touch them. He felt their evil, just as before, but this time, he looked for more. He searched for what they were...alive? Ghosts? Demon creatures? He sensed a life force within them, and knew then that they were linked to the living, even if they were not alive themselves.

He smiled, that slow, predatory smile that he'd worn for so many centuries. Where there was life, there could be death, at least when he was involved. He shoved his right hand deeper into the earth, and he took from it. He took life. He took death. He took every last breath from the earth. The dirt around his hand turned black and rotten as the earth died from his touch. His hand began to glow a bright white. Energy hummed down his arm, and his muscles went taut as he raised his head to look at the wolves.

They appeared to be swathed in a crimson hue now, and he knew his eyes were as red as theirs. The hunger inside him clawed to get free, but he kept a tight grip on it, refusing to allow it to claim his mind. He pulled his hand out of the dirt, and as he did, it vanished, disappearing from sight so that all that remained visible was the silvery, shadowy remains of his forearm, fading into nothing, an invisible weapon.

But his hand was still there, and it was deadly.

Levi stared at the wolves, waiting. His back was pressed against the rock, so that nothing could edge behind him and slip inside. His instincts howled with the urge to attack, but he fought it off, struggling to remain in control of the assassin within him. He waited. He would not strike first. *He would not become like he used to be.*

All three wolves attacked simultaneously. Levi hit the first one in the chest, and sucked every last bit of life from it in one hit. It howled in agony, and for a split second, he felt its life spiraling away from it. It wasn't an animal, but something else, a man who had once been alive, and now was truly, forever, gone. For a split second, anguish filled Levi for the man that he'd just killed, who had somehow become trapped in that hell, and then the other two latched onto him with their teeth. Poison leached into him, and his arms shriveled where their teeth were embedded. Levi cuffed the one holding onto his left arm, sucking the life out of it instantly. It shrieked and vanished, but the third one was still holding on.

He went down on his knees, fighting against the wave of weakness. He was slow, so much slower than he had once been. He fought to stay conscious as the wolf sucked his life force out of him, preying upon him exactly as he'd preyed upon so many others. Was Maya right? Was he the same? Was this what he would have become if he'd stayed with Merk?

The wolf was clamped down on his right forearm, making it impossible for him to reach it with his hand. He jammed his left hand into the dirt and sucked energy from the earth. His hand glowed and he jerked it out, pressing his finger between the shadow wolf's eyes.

It held his gaze for a moment, and he felt himself falling, sucked into their depths. His heart seemed to stop as he recognized what was coming for him. *Merk.*

Then, just as he was losing the grip on his mind, the wolf dissolved with a howl of outrage.

Levi collapsed to his knees, weakness pervading his body as he scanned their surroundings for more wolves. The night was empty and clear, and the air was warm again. The threat was gone, but he'd awoken the monster within him. It raged inside him, demanding to feed, demanding prey. The half-lives of the wolves had only whetted its appetite, not sated it. Levi dug his fingers into the dirt, his entire body straining to hold onto his sanity. "Maya," he gasped, "I need your help."

She was there beside him instantly, her hands on his shoulders. "Levi, Oh, God, what happened? Your arm is shriveled. Oh, God, it's like my sister. They got you." The anguish in her voice was vivid, tearing through the agonizing battle in his mind. Her touch was hot, firing up his muscles everywhere she touched, but it wasn't enough. He needed more. He needed *her*. Blood bond. He needed to blood bond with her, to ground himself in her. "Give me your hand," he said. His eyes rolled back in his head, and he knew he was losing the battle. Merk had been there. Merk had been in the wolf. Merk was there in his mind, trying to take him. The wolf had weakened him, and Merk was trying to get him. "Now!"

She set her hand in his, but his fingers wouldn't close. He collapsed onto his side, his body rigid. "Kill me," he snapped. "Now. Do it! Jesus."

"No!" She grabbed his shoulders. "You did this for me. I'm not going to let you die."

He grabbed her arm and jerked her down toward him. She landed with a thud on her knees beside him. "Look into my eyes," he growled. "Look at who I'm becoming."

She searched his face, and he knew she was seeing the red glow, the bottomless depth of bitter, merciless death. "Damn it, Levi. That's not you!"

"Do it, now."

"I heard you think of the blood bond," she said. "Will that help?"

"I don't know. I can't." He gasped, his body convulsing as he fought the need thundering through him. "You have to do it. Once it takes me, I'm unstoppable. I'll never let you kill me. I'm too fast. You have to do it before it gets me."

"You're already too fast." She held up the axe she was still carrying and swept her hand across it. He scented the coppery smell of her blood instantly, and need lurched in his stomach, a deep primal need almost as powerful as his lust for death. He rolled onto his side as she grabbed his hand and raked it across the blade.

She slammed their palms together, and their blood mixed. Need pulsed through him instantly, and his body clenched in response. *Maya!* He grabbed her around the waist and hauled her onto him. She came willingly, pressing herself against him as she kissed him.

Her mouth was hot and sensual, but not enough. Not fucking enough. He lifted their clasped hands and pressed his mouth to their mingled blood. The blood was tangy and hot on his tongue and slid down his throat like a searing burn that ate away at his flesh. Maya's eyes widened and he grabbed her and dragged her down to him.

This time, when they kissed, their mingled blood was damp on his lips and tongue, and he offered them to Maya. She accepted hungrily, and the kiss turned carnal within a split second. White-hot lust lashed through his mind, blanking out the lethal hunger that had been amassing inside him, replacing it with an insatiable craving for the woman in his arms.

He rolled her onto her back, and stripped off their pants, plunging into her wet, welcoming body without even breaking the kiss. She gasped his name, and he felt her emotions pouring into him. He was swamped by her desire, her fear, her passion, and her unbridled desperation for him. He pumped harder and faster, unable to get deep enough or close enough to take the edge off the intensity of the emotions raging through him. And then, just as he thought he was going to crack, the words came, the words he didn't know, and yet somehow came alive within him. *Mine to you. Yours to me. Bonded by blood, by spirit and by soul, we are one. No distance too far, no enemy too powerful, no sacrifice too great. I will always find you. I will always protect you. No matter what the cost. I am yours as you are mine.* He gave her the words, his heart, and his soul, and then hung, suspended in fear as he waited for the reply that he knew had to come, knowing, somehow, that if she didn't say them back, all would be lost for him forever.

Her voice filled his mind, so tender and beautiful he felt as if the sun had plunged right through the blackness of his soul and cast light upon it. *Mine to you. Yours to me. Bonded by blood, by spirit and by soul, we are one. No distance too far, no enemy too powerful, no sacrifice too great. I will always find you. I will always keep you safe. No matter what the cost. I am yours as you are mine.*

Maya. Her name burst through him like a great light, and then he thrust again. The orgasm exploded through him, and she clung to him, whispering his name over and over and over again into his mind as his orgasm swept her up, mixing them together into a glorious, exulting victory of connection, hurtling them over the edge into a final, joined climax.

Chapter 8

Maya's forearms started burning before Levi had even withdrawn from her body. She knew more lines were forming on her arms, marking her with his brand, and it felt so right. She needed that bond with him, and she knew there was no other future for her other than to be with him, on every level, no matter what happened. Perhaps their time together would be short. If so, she accepted it. Short was better than never having experienced the beauty of their connection.

She was trembling, a shivering that was originating from somewhere deep inside her. Levi pulled her into his arms and rested his forehead against hers. She realized that he was also trembling, and his skin was cold. She wrapped her arms around him, holding him close. There was so much to say, but at the same time, no words needed to be exchanged. She'd felt his battle with the predator within him, and she knew how strong it was, and how close it had come to taking him.

Her sudden understanding of how much he'd been willing to sacrifice for her made her hold him tighter. "Thank you," she whispered. "No one has ever risked his life for me like that."

"They were alive," he said, burying his face in her neck, as if he needed the comfort of her touch as much as she needed his. "The wolves. They weren't spirits. They had once been men. I killed them."

There was so much to his words. It meant he'd satisfied his half of the death stage by killing on her behalf. No wonder her arms were burning. They'd just done so many stages. All that was left was transference, and her half of the trust stage and death stages. The Calydon bond was trapping them, but she knew he hadn't saved her because of the *sheva* bond. He'd saved her because he was a man of honor. He'd pushed himself to the limit, and chosen to die instead of staying alive to fulfill his mission to kill Lord William.

He bowed his head, nestling more intimately against her. "They were trapped in the wolves," he said, his voice rough and harsh. "I could feel it. They were like me."

She frowned. "What?"

"They're Merk's. They had the same power I have." He lifted his head to look at her. His eyes were bloodshot, and his pupils were dilated. "Merk was controlling them. He saw me. He knows I'm alive. He almost got me. They're his wolves."

His words sank into her like a cold chill. "You mean, he sent the wolves to my village? He used them to trap me? Offering respite from the creatures *he* sent to destroy us?" Nausea churned in her stomach. "Did he kill my parents?"

Levi nodded. "I think those men were once like me. I think they were my future."

She stared at him as dark dread filled her. She didn't have to ask if he was serious. She could feel the weight of his words preying upon her. "You'd be a phantom wolf now if you hadn't been imprisoned, wouldn't you?"

"Probably. Or at least, I'd be on my way."

"So, what do we do?"

He wrapped his hand around the braided bracelet on her wrist, the one that bound her to Merk no matter what. "We kill him."

"But what about the wolves? Will that stop them?" Even as she asked it, she knew his answer. "They're too far gone, aren't they? They aren't men. The hunger—it owns them, right? They won't stop, will they? Why would Rohan think they defended ancient spirits, if they are tools that Merk created?"

"I've heard of guardian spirit wolves before, but these aren't them. Merk imitated them. And I guess that they periodically cease their attacks on your kingdom only because Merk pulls them back. My guess is that he gave your parents the sunlight because he was trying to convince them to go to him for protection, just like you eventually did. When they refused, he decided to take them out."

"Oh, God." She felt sick, so violently ill that she'd trusted the man who had set the scourge on her kingdom.

"Once he's dead, there will be no one holding them back." Levi inhaled deeply, and pressed his face to her neck again. "I never thought I'd be sane again," he said softly. "You brought me back. I can't tell you what it feels like to lie here with you, to feel your skin against mine, and to know that I'm not streaking across the countryside, hunting for someone to kill."

She hugged him more tightly, threading her fingers through his hair. "The blood bond is amazing, isn't it?"

"Yeah." He lifted his head to look at her. His brow was furrowed. "Tell me your darkest secret."

"The trust stage," she whispered.

He nodded. "Merk is hunting us now. He'll find us soon. I need all your strength if I'm going to resist him. We need to finish the bond."

She swallowed. "But once we finish it, we're destined to lose all that matters to us. I don't want to lose my kingdom." She paused. "Or you," she whispered.

"I fucking hate having my life dictated to me," he said. "I lived that way for a century, and I'm done with it. I'm not going to be controlled by a psychopath, or some shitty destiny." His face became fierce. "Somewhere along the line, the *sheva* bond got twisted into something bad and destructive, but we've already seen how good and powerful it really is. Having someone you can count on no matter what is the only thing worth living for, and I refuse to believe that it'll force us to betray each other. We both know how dark things can get, and we won't go back there. *I won't let it happen.*"

Warmth spread through her at his words, and she smiled. "Okay."

He raised his brows. "Okay? Just like that, you're willing to blow off a thousand years of *sheva* destiny?"

"Yep. I like your version better, and I know that we're both stubborn enough to pull it off."

He grinned. "That's my woman." He kissed her, hard

and deep, until she felt him growing hard inside her again. With a low growl, he broke the kiss. "As much as I want to make love to you right now, we don't have much time. Tell me your darkest secret. Trust me with something you've never trusted anyone with before. Or give me the power to kill you. Either way works."

She raised her brows, trying to think of something. "Just by being with you, you have the power to kill me. You don't think that works?"

"No. It has to be a specific action." He kissed her again, and began moving his hips. *Talk to me, woman. Now. What's the one thing you don't want to tell me, and then spill it.*

She arched back, her body tightening as her belly clenched with desire once again. *That's not fair. You're distracting me.*

I'm a man on a mission. No time for fair. Talk. He thrust deeper, and she yelped as desire rushed through her. *You're avoiding. Tell me.*

She gripped Levi's shoulders, moving her hips under his. "I don't have any deep, dark secrets," she said. "I don't know what to say."

He moved deeper, and her body clenched with need. *There has to be something you don't want to say, something you fear putting out there, something you feel like if you said it, you might shatter.*

She opened her eyes to look at him, and she saw the hunger in them, not hunger for death, hunger for her. Her heart tightened, and her eyes suddenly filled with tears. No one had ever looked at her like that, as if she were the only thing that mattered. She had always been second class in her family, an afterthought that wasn't important. She'd tried so hard to get them to love her, but no one ever had. She'd told them she loved them a thousand times, but never once had they said it back, until she'd finally learned it was easier not to say it, than to have those three words hanging out there unacknowledged.

But Levi had put her first. He'd sacrificed himself and his dreams to save hers. He made her feel like the most important woman in the world... Suddenly, she knew her secret, the words she would never be brave enough to utter.

He stopped moving his hips, searching her face. *What is it?*

She bit her lip, looking past him at the night that was so dark. Not even a star lit up the evening, and she knew it was because of the shadow wolves hunting them, getting close.

Levi caught her jaw and directed her gaze back to her face. "You have to say it," he said. "You have to say it now."

She became aware of a chill in the air, and she knew more wolves were coming. But there was something else. Something more deadly. Something that made the braided band on her wrist tighten. "Merk's coming now, isn't he? For us?"

"Yeah." Levi didn't move away, and he didn't withdraw from her body. He just waited, infinite patience, for her.

She framed his face with her hands, his whiskers prickling his fingers. "My secret," she whispered. "Is..." She stopped. "I know you don't want to hear this, and I'm not asking anything of you. I'd never say it if I didn't have to—"

He laughed softly, a deep chuckle that seemed to reverberate through her. "Just say it, Maya."

"I love you."

His face went blank, and his body went utterly still. Silence arose between them, and she felt that same desolation rise inside her as she'd felt so many times in her life when she'd said those words, and they'd been met with silence. She managed a smile and held up her arm, which was burning. "It worked," she said, pretending she didn't care that he hadn't said it back. "More lines."

He turned his head to her arm, and, to her surprise, pressed a long kiss against her flesh. He said nothing, but the tenderness of his kiss seemed to ease the desolation racing through her. He hadn't used words, but his action was significant. He hadn't turned away from her or rejected her. He'd kissed the mark that bound them, a deep, searing kiss that she knew said the words that he hadn't spoken. Maybe not that he loved her, but that he accepted her love, and would treasure it forever. It was more than she'd ever gotten, and she knew it was all he could offer.

She nodded, silent, unable to speak over the swell of emotion forming in her throat.

"One and a half stages left," he said, running his hand over her arm. "Your half of the death stage and calling my weapon."

She swallowed and took a breath. "I really don't want to kill anyone."

He met her gaze, and there were hundreds of years in regret in his eyes. "I don't want you to have to live through that. We're tight now. Maybe it will be enough."

The wind began to whistle through the trees, an ancient howling sound that sent chills down her spine. "He's almost here," she whispered.

"That he is." Levi kissed her again, hard and fast, and then finally, pulled out of her. His absence left behind a gaping hole in her soul, and for a minute, a lifetime of isolation surged back over her. Then he gave her a wink, and the tension vanished. He was still hers, no matter what. Forever.

Within a split second, he already had his pants back in place, but he had no shoes or shirt. Just himself and his axes. His body was lean, but taut with muscle. He looked ready and lethal, a warrior who wasn't afraid to do whatever he had to do. "You ready for battle, sweetheart?"

"No. I still can't call your weapon." She sat up and grabbed for her jeans, glancing around at the dark night as she quickly got dressed. There was no time left to develop battle skills she'd never had. "So, what's our plan?" The air was icy cold now, and the bracelet on her wrist was getting even tighter.

"We have to find out where he got the sunlight from."

She grabbed Levi's arm. "Don't kill him until we find it. We can't let his wolves kill my kingdom."

He looked at her. "He can't be allowed to go free, Maya. That's the bottom line."

"But—" She caught her breath as two sets of gleaming red eyes appeared in the trees behind him. "They're here." As Levi spun around, two wolves stepped out of the darkness, their muzzles almost translucent as the shadows swirled through their bodies. Their eyes settled right on her, and the back of her neck prickled.

Levi knelt beside her and placed his right hand on the earth. "If there's only two, I can take them."

The wolves didn't move, however. They simply kept staring at her, until their faces began to shift and blur. She blinked, trying to clear her vision, but the faces continued to morph before her eyes. "Levi? Is it just me, or—"

"No, it's not." He was still crouched beside her, and the earth was blackened around his hand. "They're shifting."

She dug her fingers into his shoulders. "They look human."

"They were human before. They're floating between the two worlds." He stood up, using his left hand to clasp her wrist and draw her behind him. "Don't be fooled by them. They're not human anymore."

A cold chill raced down Maya's spine as one of the wolves flashed into a full human face for a split second. She saw a face with the same blue eyes that she had, cheekbones that were high and refined, and a cool arrogance that she'd lived with her whole life. "Oh, God, Did you see that?"

"A woman, yeah." Levi suddenly glanced at her. "She looked like you."

Maya's legs started to shake. "It's my mother. That wolf... it's my mother." As she spoke, she jerked her gaze to the other wolf. Again, a human face flashed into visibility, and she saw the peppery beard of her father for a split second before the wolf took over again. She gripped Levi's wrist. "It's my parents. When the wolves came the first time, they took their souls, they—"

"They are not your parents." He tightened his grip on her wrist as the wolves circled closer, their teeth bared.

"Don't kill them," she whispered, her voice stark with terror. *Please, Levi, please.*

Levi swore at the anguish in her voice, watching the wolves close in. He pulled Maya behind him, his hand pulsing with the energy to kill. *Maya, they're gone. They aren't your parents—*

They will always be my parents.

As she spoke, there was movement behind the two wolves. The shadows seemed to part as a man emerged from the darkness wearing a calf-length, leather coat and a black shirt. Long, blond hair strayed over his shoulders, and his elegant fingers were wrapped around the handle of an old sword. His face regal and impassive, just as it always had been.

Merk. Levi went still, his heart pounding as he watched the man who had ruled him for so long appear. Levi moved in front of Maya, using his body to block her as Merk stopped. He felt the weight of his gaze on him, and in his mind. Levi immediately reinforced his mental shields to block him. Everything inside him screamed with the instinct to launch himself at the other man before he could attack, and he shifted his weight—

Maya put her hand on his back, her fingers cold against his skin, and he stilled, barely able to think over the blood thundering through his mind. *Give me a chance, Levi.*

It was against everything he believed, but he stayed still, and he didn't stop her as she stepped around him so she could be seen by Merk. "Lord William," she said, her voice clear and regal.

"Lady Maya." His blue eyes flicked toward her with a predatory interest that made Levi's lip curl. "You have come to seal our deal."

"I have."

"Come to me," Merk said, his voice cool and tempting.

Don't take one step, Levi warned her. *If he touches you, I'll kill him. I swear I will.*

Don't kill him, she snapped at him, but she stayed by his side. "First, I need to know the safety of my people is assured," she said to Merk, her voice steady and calm.

"It is. I am bound by the bargain just as you are." He held out his hand. "Come." His voice carried a bit of a push, and he felt Maya's resistance ebb.

Stay. He reached out with his mind and wrapped her in his protective shield, bringing her into his defenses.

Merk's gaze flickered toward Levi. "Do not interfere, son."

Son? Maya's surprise surged through him. *He's your father?*

He claimed the role, but he isn't my father. But for years, Merk had played that role, fulfilling the fantasies of an orphan kid who longed for his roots. Levi had believed Merk was his dad, who had tracked him down at the orphanage and rescued him. He'd done everything he could to win his favor, and thought it was his fault whenever the bastard had beat the hell out of him to train him. It wasn't until later, much later, that he realized the truth, but by then, Merk's grip on him was too unassailable. It hadn't mattered then. But it mattered now.

He watched as Merk slid his hand into the pocket of his cloak, and he tensed, knowing they had only a split second until Merk acted. "You have three seconds to tell Maya where the power source is, or you die."

Merk raised his brows."I don't fear you, son. You could never turn on me."

Levi narrowed his eyes. "Two seconds."

Maya gripped his arm. *Don't do this, Levi. You haven't given us time!*

Watch his hand, Maya. Don't take your eyes off it. "One."

Merk moved his hand, Levi started to lunge for him, and then something sharp sank into the back of his neck. He reached behind him, vaguely aware of Maya's shout, but it was too late. His body seemed to fragment as he fell, and he hit the earth with a thud, unable to move, to think, to breathe, and unable to fight off the darkness as it sucked him down.

Chapter 9

"Levi!" Maya gasped as Levi collapsed beside her, then she saw two wolves on his back, their teeth sunk deep into his neck, sucking the life out of him, just as they'd done to her sister. For a split second, she was frozen in terror as memories of that horrible night came back to her, and then she saw Levi's skin turning black and beginning to shrivel, just as had happened to her sister and her parents. *Her parents were killing Levi.* "No!" She screamed in protest and lunged for them. There was a crack and a flash of black light, and then Levi's axe was in her hand. She swung it through the wolves, who howled and vanished, reforming a yard away, their teeth snarling and their red eyes flashing.

Levi didn't move, and she straddled him, her feet braced and the axe ready. As she stood there, she felt her arms burning as more lines were added to the brand. Now that she had claimed his weapon, their ties were even tighter.

Deep possessiveness rolled through her, a need to protect Levi and defend him. "Don't touch him," she said, tightening her grip on his weapon. She could barely breathe through the horror that she had just tried to kill her parents to defend Levi. What kind of choice had that been? Was that the *sheva* bond, making her choose a man instead of her family? Her stomach turned, but she didn't lower the weapon. She *couldn't* lower the weapon. Levi was lying on the ground between her feet, rasping for breath, and there was no way on this earth she would step away from him and leave him to be killed. "Make it stop," she shouted at Merk, who was watching the whole thing with a smile on his face. "Save him."

"My dear, what would you give for me to save him?" Merk walked around in a leisurely circle, trailing his fingers over the heads of the wolves who had once been her parents. "A kingdom, perhaps? You have already given me that. Your servitude? Already claimed. Your body? At my mercy."

She saw the merciless cruelty in his eyes, and her stomach congealed. "My body wasn't part of the deal." She'd known he would try to take it, but it hadn't been part of the deal.

"You are mine," he said. "Mine, in any way I see fit." His gaze swept over her. "You will be begging for mercy before the night is out." He held up his arm, where a matching wristband glistened in the moonlight. "The moment I save your kingdom, you become mine. You have nothing left to bargain with."

Her mouth became dry with fear. "You endangered my kingdom. You sent the wolves after us. You created danger that I'm trying to save them from."

"Of course I did." Merk laughed caustically, a grating sound that felt like razor blades across her flesh. "It was my kingdom, and my brother stole it. It's mine, now, as will be his daughter."

She stared at him as his words sank in. "You're...my dad's brother?" Her father had always said his brother had died when they were young...but he hadn't?

Lord William nodded. "I'm the younger brother. Number two. Worth nothing in his eyes. Just like you."

Just like her? Number two? Worth nothing in her father's eyes? His words were so familiar, words she'd said and felt a thousand times. "I'm not like you," she whispered.

"No? I lost my inheritance to my brother, just like how you lost it to your sister. Were they worthy? No. You were the one who figured out how to save the kingdom, not any of them. You're the worthy one, just like me. I claimed the kingdom." He spat at the wolf beside him, and then clipped it on the head. It vanished beneath his touch, and reformed a few yards away, its red eyes still fixated on Maya. "And now it's mine, and so are you."

He was her uncle? Bile churned in her stomach, but she

clenched her jaw, trying to work through all the implications. All her complaints about being the second born seemed so stupid now. She didn't want to be like him, consumed by the baggage of her birth order. She had to stop him. She had to find out how to save things. "How did you channel the wolves? How do you own them?"

He shrugged. "I harvested Levi's magic to create more assassins, but the power consumed them. I was left with a bunch of rotting corpses that were useless to me, until I realized how handy they were for assaulting my brother's kingdom. They're like Levi. I point them to a target, and they go. It's easy to convince them that the kingdom is under attack from the people, and they need to protect it. They're great warriors, but I have figured out how to distort their perception of reality. Each time they attack, they add to their numbers with victims, though it takes time for them to fully shift. That's why it's taken so damn long to make this happen. But soon, I'll have enough to take on targets that have actually figured out how to defend themselves, unlike the defenseless kingdom my brother ruled so pathetically."

Chills clenched her spine. Had he used the wolves against other targets? Had he sucked the life from other people? How many people would he try to destroy? "But the sunlight stops them, doesn't it?"

He nodded. "Shuts 'em down forever. I had to create something to control them, to teach them that I was in charge. And it's not sunlight. You're such a fool. You actually think I could harvest sunlight? It's magic, girl, just magic, encased in a stone." He smiled. "Ironically, I buried a stash of it at the castle. It's there, the secret to saving it all, and you never knew. I always enjoyed that little irony."

She felt sick. How could she have trusted this man? How could she possibly have bound herself to him? "You killed my parents," she whispered.

He made a sound of disgust. "I killed my brother. I wanted your mother for myself, but she went down with him." He swiped his fingers through the wolf that was her mother. "So, I tried for your sister, and she was too pathetic and weak. Now, it's just you." He smiled and held up his wrist. "And now you're mine."

She didn't need him anymore. The secret to protecting the kingdom was already at the castle. All she had to do was find it. "Where is the light? How do I find it?"

He laughed softly. "Wrong question, Maya. Wrong fucking question." He smiled, a haunting, horrific smile. "It's in the dungeon under the north tower, buried a hundred feet deep and encased in steel. Pull it out, and the wolves will stop."

Elation rushed through her. "I don't need you anymore—" She raised the axe to attack, and then, suddenly, the bracelet tightened around her wrist. It jerked her forward off her feet, and dragged her to her knees before him. "What?"

Merk grabbed her hair and yanked her head back. "When I told you where it was, I saved your kingdom from the wolves. I fulfilled my part of the bargain, and now you're mine." He dragged her to her feet, and she gasped in pain. She tried to swing the axe to cut him down, but it bounced off him. Horrified, she watched it dissolve from her hands. "You can't hurt me," he laughed. "You swore fealty to me. Fealty means you don't kill me." He fisted her hair even more aggressively, sending shards of pain through her. "It means you have nothing but utmost loyalty to me."

She gasped in pain. "The kingdom isn't safe yet. Just because you told me—"

"Of course it is. You're the queen. You have the information. Call your people. Tell them where to find it. The deal is done." His gaze dropped to her breasts. "And now, my brother's daughter is about to pay for his betrayal."

Bile churned through her stomach. *Levi! Wake up! I need you.* She'd gotten what she needed from Merk, but was it too late? Had she pushed it too far? *Levi!*

There was a stirring behind her, and she twisted in Merk's grasp as Levi stumbled to his feet. His skin was still blackened and shriveled, but it was already filling out and healing. Relief rushed through her, until she saw his eyes.

His pupils were dilated, turning his eyes into black pits…except for the red glow emanating from them, just like her parents. He was staring at Merk like an automaton. His face was blank, as if the person within him was gone.

Merk pointed at Levi. "Elisabeth Brennan. Finish her

off."

Her sister? He was sending Levi to kill her sister? "No!" She fought against his grip, gasping at the pain as he jerked her hair mercilessly. "Levi, no! Don't do this! Don't!"

An expression of raw hunger raked across Levi's face, and she realized now that Merk had given him a target, he was ready to feed on it. "No!" She slammed her elbow up and back toward Merk's throat, but he easily evaded her blow and shoved her face into the dirt.

She gagged on the dirt, trying to turn her head so she could breathe. *Levi!* How could he stand there and watch this? How could Merk's control of his mind be so tight on him that Levi wouldn't feel the need to protect her? *I'm your* sheva, *for God's sake! Your job is to save me!* For once in her life, she knew where she stood with someone. She *knew* she was Levi's priority. *Levi!*

She turned her head enough to get her face out of the dirt. Levi was staring at her, as if trying to figure out who she was. She reached out with her mind to touch his, but there was none of his warmth left. No emotion. Just a raging hunger for death. He was gone. *Oh, God, Levi. What happened?* Tears bled down her cheeks as she opened her mind to him. *Please, Levi. I need you.*

He stared at her blankly, not taking his gaze off her.

"Go," Merk snapped. "Now. Elisabeth needs to be dead before I turn the light back on in the kingdom."

Again, Levi didn't move. He just kept staring at her, as if willing her to do something. And then, she realized what it was. The bond wasn't complete. The connection wasn't strong enough yet to allow him to defeat Merk's hold on him. She had to finish it. The death stage was all that was left. Who could she kill? The bracelet kept her from killing Merk. She'd never kill Levi. All that were left were the two snarling wolves, her parents.

She stared at them in horror. How could she kill them? Her parents?

But even as she thought it, she could hear them, telling her that nothing was as important as saving the kingdom. It was her job to sacrifice herself to save it. If that meant killing her own parents, then so be it.

She saw Levi's hand, blackened from the dirt, and she knew that was her weapon to call. Not his axe. His hand. With his power, she could kill her parents, just like he'd killed the other wolves.

She looked up at Merk, and his hateful visage. So much death and destruction over a village? She'd lost her parents to that kingdom long before they'd died, as well as her sister. Would she lose them again by killing them? How much more was she willing to give for a village and for duty?

She looked at Levi, and the haunted look on his face, and she knew the cost that so many deaths had caused him. How could she let him live with the life he'd been thrust back into? Merk would be dead now, if she'd let Levi kill him when they'd first arrived. Merk would be dead, Levi would be free, and together maybe they would have figured out her uncle's plans and somehow saved the kingdom. The solution had been at the castle the whole time, and she'd been too blind to see it. Because of her foolishness, she'd forced Levi to relive his worst nightmare, she'd trapped herself with Merk, her sister was going to die, and Merk was going to claim the kingdom. Everything she'd fought against was lost, all because she'd been so blinded by trying to be worthy of her birthright.

She finally understood the enormity of the sacrifice she'd made for her kingdom, the same one her parents had made, the same ones her sister had made: sacrificing the people they loved for the kingdom. Was it never ending? Where was the line? What were the choices? Kill her parents for a village? When did it stop?

"Now, Levi," Merk commanded. "*Now!*"

With one final stare, Levi tore his gaze off her and turned away. He began to jog toward the trees, away from her, toward her kingdom, toward the world that had brought only grief. As he loped away, she heard his voice in her head, so faint, as if he could barely summon the words. *You promised.*

Promised? What had she promised? Then she realized what he was saying. She'd promised to kill him. She'd promised not to let him go back to that life. The tattoo on his hip.

She looked back at Merk, who was grinning. She looked at her parents, sitting beside him, snarling with their red eyes and ghostly figure.

If she killed her parents, the *sheva* bond would be completed, giving Levi the strength to break Merk's hold, but then her parents would be dead, and Levi would be destined to go insane and destroy everything that mattered to her.

But if she killed Levi, he would die, she'd kill herself, and Merk would still be in control of her and her kingdom.

She couldn't kill Merk, no matter how hard she tried.

God, what was she supposed to do?

Levi leapt into the woods, and disappeared from sight, racing toward her sister to finish her off. Maya's heart seemed to congeal in her chest. "No!" She screamed in protest, and then his axe appeared in her hand. It was glowing with a black light, and she knew it was laced with his deadly magic, enough to kill the wolves.

She whirled around toward her parents, but just as she raised the axe, she knew there was no way she would ever strike a blow against them. To kill someone she loved would destroy her. She swung toward Merk. "I will *never* be like you."

He laughed, a ghostly, creepy cackle. "By doing nothing, you already are—"

"No!" She screamed the denial, and knew what she had to do. There was one more way to complete the bond and free Levi and her kingdom. *I love you, Levi.*

And then, she turned the axe toward herself and plunged it into her stomach. She screamed with agony as the blade sunk into her abdomen, and fell to her knees as Merk shouted at her and grabbed her arms. The wolves howled with rage, and she laughed as she crumbled to the earth. "I win," she gasped. "*You lose.*"

Maya! Levi's clear, anguished roar tore through her mind, and she smiled through her pain.

He was back.

She'd done it. Death had sealed their bond, and freed him. Everyone she loved would be safe. Finally, she'd done something right. The world began to spin as a black cloud began to take over her mind. *Kill Merk. The sunlight is buried under the west tower. I love you.* She vaguely recalled that the *sheva* bond required that Levi go insane and destroy everything that mattered, that he wasn't supposed to save her kingdom.

But he would.

She knew it.

He was just that stubborn.

⌗ ⌗ ⌗

Maya's pain tore through Levi like a tsunami, flooding him with emotions and terror, shattering the hold Merk had on his mind. Instant awareness illuminated his mind, and he whirled around, sprinted back toward where he'd left his woman. *Maya! Hang on! I'm coming for you!*

Fear hammered at him, a terror so deep he could barely breathe. He couldn't lose her. *Maya!* He burst from the woods and saw Maya on the ground at Merk's feet. The bastard had Maya by the wrist and was screaming at her.

The moment Levi saw Merk threatening Maya, something inside him roared to life. The beast he'd fought off for so long tore free, and he let it go. He embraced it as he called out his weapons with a crack and a flash of black light. While he was still a hundred yards away, he unleashed them in a one-two assault. Merk looked up a split second before the weapons hit, but he had no time to move.

The blades sliced clean through him *without causing any damage.* He'd become like his wolves. Impossible to kill.

Fuck impossible. Levi hated that word.

He charged across the clearing, and Merk sprang to his feet to face him. *Levi. You are mine. You will stop.*

Merk pushed at Levi's mind, and he felt the same pressure that had controlled him for so long, but it didn't matter anymore. Maya was down. She needed him. And this fucking beast was in his way. *This was his next target.* His mind laser-focused on Merk the way it used to focus on his targets so long ago, a ruthless, single-minded mission that would not be averted. His entire being went still, and his footsteps became silent. He became hyper-aware. He could hear every beat of Merk's heart. He could hear the rush of his blood through his veins. He could smell every drop of sweat as it trickled down his spine. He tasted his fear, his sudden awareness that he had become the target.

Stop, Levi! I order you! Elisabeth is your target!

The command drifted past Levi, not even touching his consciousness. There was no power, nothing that could trump the depth of Levi's need to protect his woman. He streaked across the clearing, so fast he was nothing but a blur. He saw Merk's eyes widen, his pupils dilate, and his nostrils flare. And then, he began to run.

It was too late. Too little. Too nothing.

Levi clasped Merk on the shoulder, and gave to the man all that he'd forced Levi to give to so many people over so many centuries. Merk stumbled, and went down to his knees, gasping for breath.

Levi eased down beside him, his hand still on the man's shoulder. His entire soul was screaming with the need to finish it, to kill him, to wipe the last bit of life from his soul. Hunger tore through him, a blindness that seemed to consume him. The world turned crimson as a darker, more visceral rage took over. In the darkest recesses of his mind, Levi realized he had crossed that line. He was becoming a rogue Calydon warrior, just as fate decreed would happen. His upper lip curled in disgust, as he dragged Merk across the ground, his weapon clenched in his hand, his need for destruction growing and expanding. Not just Merk. For it all—

Merk gasped, staring up at him. "Have mercy."

The word slithered past him, not even registering. Mercy meant nothing to him. Mercy was—

Levi. The kingdom. You have to save it for me.

Maya's voice burst through the white-hot need raging through him. The rage and fury gripping him so tight fragmented, and he whirled around. Through the blood-red haze, he saw Maya on the ground, trying to drag herself over to him. She was still alive!

His killing frenzy shattered instantly at the sight of Maya trying to crawl toward him, until all that was left was her. Her need for him flooded him, filling him with her very soul. He dropped Merk instantly, not even caring what happened to the man he'd wanted to kill for so long. All that mattered was that his woman needed him. *Maya!* He raced over to her and pulled her into his arms. Her shirt was thick with blood, her face was ashen, and her skin was turning black. His heart seemed to stop in his chest, and he pulled her into his arms. Her heart was barely beating, and he knew that she had only moments left to live. *I have you, sweetheart. I promise.* He tucked her against him and placed his hand over her heart, pouring his Calydon healing energy into her. He tapped into their bond, opening himself to her.

Her heartbeat was faint and fading fast, slipping out of his grip faster than he could hold onto. Fear beat through him, and he secured his hold on her. *Come on, Maya! Stay with me.*

Her head rested against his chest. *You broke destiny. You're sane. You did it.* Her mind was so faint, and he knew he was losing her.

I couldn't go rogue. I still had a chance to save you. I didn't have time to go destroy the world. You're my life, Maya. You're my everything. He had to go into the healing sleep. It was where his powers were the strongest. He glanced around, and saw Merk sprawled on the ground, unconscious, but not dead. The wolves paced around him. It wasn't safe. It wasn't fucking safe to go to sleep.

Fuck it.

Without her, nothing mattered.

He'd rather die trying.

Come with me. He closed his eyes and laid back on the ground, tucking her more intimately against him, so they were tightly entwined, creating as much physical connection as he could. He called to the power of his sleep, and it came immediately, enfolding him in the deep, powerful pulsating energy of healing. He pulled Maya into it with him, and it enveloped them both. It swirled through him, and he thrust it into Maya, giving her every last bit of the strength he had. He reached inside her with his energy, trying to knit the damage she'd done to herself, but it was so deep, so ragged. He worked feverishly to try to heal the damaged blood vessels, but his own poison was still ravaging her body, shutting her down cell by cell. Shit. He didn't have enough. He couldn't heal both injuries at the same time. It was too much. *Maya!*

Then, suddenly, he felt another presence. A heavy hand touched his shoulder, and a male presence mingled with his. *Let me in. I can help.*

Levi was shocked by the realization that Rohan was there, offering his healing. He didn't argue. He didn't bother to ask how the ancient warrior had tracked them down. He simply opened a channel between them. Rohan's powerful healing energy surged into him, ten times the strength of Levi's.

You guys are too old to do this alone. You need some youthful energy. Thano's lighter, but almost equally powerful energy flooded him as well. The three warriors worked together, their voices merging in the ancient healing chant of the Calydon warrior. Levi had never heard the chant, but when Rohan and Thano began, he seemed to know the words, his voice moving in perfect unison with the other two, their voices rising to a crescendo as the intense power of their healing energy merged together, pouring into Maya with such force that her body began to tremble.

Levi enfolded her against him, cradling her as the healing energy raced through her, taking away the damage, fighting against the death calling for her. For a long moment, the battle was waged, and he felt her spirit hovering in the balance.

She needs you, Rohan said. *Bring her back, Levi. Do it now.*

Levi tried to summon even more healing energy, but felt Thano's burst of impatience. *Tell the girl you love her, old man. We got the healing thing. You gotta give her a reason to live.*

Love her? Tell her he loved her? Rightness flooded him, and Levi bent his head and pressed a kiss against her temple. *Maya, I can't live without you. I love you with every breath I take. My need to keep you safe broke through everything that was trying to control me. It was my love for you that shattered destiny's grip on me. Do you understand how significant that is? Come back to me. I need you. You're all I've ever had, and you're all I'll ever need.* He gripped her more tightly. *I love you, Maya. Do you hear me?*

There was an agonizing moment of silence from her, and then suddenly, faintly, he felt her mind reach out to his. *Levi?*

I love you. He said the words she'd given so freely to him, the ones he'd been unable to give to her at that time. He'd been such a fool, thinking that he couldn't offer her love. The moment he thought he'd lost her, he'd known that he loved her, and he'd known that it was the kind of love he'd never have another chance to have. *I know I'm a bad choice. I can never change my past, and I'll always be a danger to the world, but—*

Her fingers wrapped around his, cutting him off. Her touch was warm and tender, so much softer than he had a right to experience. But he closed his fingers around hers, holding her hand. *I love you, too, Levi. I need you to be who you are. I suck at battle. One of us has to be the protector.*

His heart lifted, almost dancing in his chest, and he felt like his world had come to a complete stop. She loved him. She knew what he was, and *she loved him.* After a lifetime of hating everything he was, for the first time, he knew there was a purpose to his life, a reason for his skills: to protect the woman he loved.

Chapter 10

"It's here."

Maya's heart leapt as Levi held up an ancient, iron chest with a rusted padlock. He was at the bottom of a hole more than thirty feet deep, accompanied by Rohan and Thano, who had helped him dig. The rest of Rohan's team was still out in the kingdom, fighting off the wolves. Merk was in their dungeon, unconscious, but alive, but his near demise hadn't resulted in the wolves ceasing their attacks. Somehow, he'd convinced them they needed to protect the castle, and now they no longer needed him to feed their aggression. The battle was getting fierce, and only Levi's ability to fend them off had allowed the four of them to get to the base of the west tower, where the wolves were the most numerous and most dangerous.

The only wolves who weren't attacking were her parents, who had shadowed them the whole way, snarling at any wolves who tried to attack Maya. The sky was dark and Rohan's team was exhausted. They were almost out of time.

Levi handed the chest up to Rohan, who was still wearing his cloak despite having been digging relentlessly for several hours. Thano, on the other hand, had stripped down to his jeans, tossing his shirt aside as he dug, his long-handled shovels allowing him to dig from his horse's back. The muscles in his upper body were ripped, but his legs were still and lifeless where they were strapped to his saddle.

Rohan passed the chest up to Thano, who set it over the front of his saddle, and urged Apollo up the side of the pit that they'd dug so quickly. Apollo leapt up over the edge of the hole, landing beside Maya. The horse went down on his knees, and Thano leaned over to set the chest on the ground beside Maya.

She put her hands on the chest, but it was cold and dark. "I don't feel anything." She looked up as Levi climbed out of the hole beside her. "What if he was lying?"

"We'll know soon enough." Levi called out his axe with a crack and a flash of black light. He put his hand on her shoulder to pull her back, and then he swung hard, slamming the blade of his axe into the padlock. Sparks flew through the air, and then the lock clattered to the ground.

Maya lunged for it, and unhooked the latch. She grabbed it, but it didn't move. "It's rusted." Levi grabbed it with her, but it didn't move.

Silently, without bothering with words, Thano and Rohan moved up beside him. The three warriors wedged their weapons under the rim of the chest in silent, automatic teamwork. "On three," Levi shouted. "One. Two. Three!"

Moving as one, the three of them leaned on their weapons. There was a loud grinding sound, and then the lid popped open. Light blinded them, and Maya covered her eyes as the rays filled the small cavern. The wolves snarled, and then vanished, disappearing into the air.

Dear God, it was the light. It worked. They'd found it. Disbelief rushed through her, followed by elation. She fell to her knees, too stunned to stand. "We did it," she whispered. "Oh, my God, Levi, *we did it.*"

"Of course we did. Impossible means nothing, right?" As he spoke, she felt his pain as the sunlight hit his eyes, which were still sensitive to light of that intensity.

She leapt to her feet and reached for him. He caught her hand, turning toward her as he kept his arm over his eyes.

"Thano, get it up to the top of the tower where it can shine on the kingdom," Rohan commanded. "Set it on the top of the roof."

Thano swept a large, white stone out of the chest. He balanced it on the pommel of his saddle, and Apollo took off at a gallop, his hooves clattering as he raced for the stairs.

She looked around, and saw the wolves that were her

parents standing by the door. They were the only ones still present, and their eyes were no longer red. She saw the blue eyes of her mother and the dark brown of her father. Hope leapt through her. "Mom? Dad?"

Then, as she watched, they slowly disappeared, disintegrating into the air. "No!" She lunged for them, but her fingers slipped through empty air as she lost her parents for the second time. "No—"

Levi's strong arms wrapped around her, drawing her against his body. *I'm sorry, sweetheart, but at least they're not trapped anymore. They're able to move on.* His words were so genuine and warm, enfolding around her and giving her the comfort she'd longed for her entire life.

She wasn't alone anymore, even without her parents. Maybe that had been their job, to bring her to him. She pulled back to look at him, and saw his eyes were still scrunched shut against the light, even though it had faded significantly. "Levi." She placed her hand over his eyes, shielding them from the light.

Thank you. He slid his hand through her hair, drawing her head toward him for a kiss. They'd been in such a rush to get back to the kingdom, that they hadn't had time for a moment of intimacy. This was the first kiss they'd shared since their bond had been completed, and it was a thousand times sweeter than it had ever been before. She felt his love, his kindness, and his commitment to her. It was deep in his soul, a part of his heart, a promise of forever, a promise that she gave right back to him.

She wrapped her arms around his neck, kissing him more deeply—

Rohan cleared his throat.

Maya pulled back immediately, but Levi kept his arm around her, not letting her go. She felt his pain when she pulled her hand from his eyes, and she immediately went back to his side, covering his eyes. She could tell that the light had damaged the fragile healing of his eyes, and he would have to start over.

She turned to face Rohan, who was standing before them, his hood still casting his face in shadows. "Thank you for your help."

He nodded.

Levi wrapped his arm more tightly around her. "Why

did you come to help me save her?" he asked. "Why were you there?"

"Because we never completed our deal," Rohan said, not quite answering the question. "You promised to blood bond with me and become a part of the Order of the Blade. It's time for you to become one of us."

For a long moment, Levi didn't move, and he didn't answer. He'd spent his life at the mercy of Merk, and he'd learned that the only way to survive was by himself. Except...he hadn't survived on his own. It had taken Maya and both Calydons to free him and break him from the curse that had bound him for so long. It had taken a team to save Maya.

"We need you," Rohan said. "I need you. There are some creatures even I cannot defeat. But you have a gift, and there are times I will need to call upon it."

"A gift?" His curse was a gift? Levi fisted his hand, the one that had caused so much death and owned him so completely for so long, the one that had been nothing more than a curse and a trap. And yet, with Maya by his side and in his heart, he'd been able to control it, and to maintain his own sanity. He'd used it for good, and he'd been able to stop himself when he chose. Was it possible he could use it for something good? To reclaim himself from all the damage he'd caused for so long?

Hope, the first hope in so long, began to shimmer inside him. Maya slipped her hand in his, and he brought their joined hands to his lips, pressing a kiss to her fingers. *What do you think, sweetheart? I can't do it without you. You keep me sane.*

Pride glowed in her voice. *I think you'd make a great Order of the Blade warrior. You're a hero, Levi, not a bad guy.*

He grinned and pulled her hand off his eyes, needing to see her. She was smiling at him, her face so soft with love that his heart turned over. *You believe in me.*

Of course I do. You're worth believing in. Join the Order, Levi. If there was ever a warrior worthy of the mantle, it's you.

He grinned. *Have I told you how amazing you are?*

Not in so many words. Feel free to spend forever thinking of ways to tell me.

He chuckled, happiness spilling through him.

Happiness. Who in hell's name would have ever thought he'd be happy? But he was. And it was awesome. He wrapped his arm around her and glanced across the cavern. His eyes still hurt, but he was able to squint enough to make out the shadowy visage of Rohan. "Yeah, okay. I'm in, but only if Maya comes with me. I don't trust myself without her."

Rohan nodded. "I accept those terms." His voice softened. "Despite what the Calydon tradition claims, sometimes women make us stronger, and the loss of them torments us forever." He called out his sword with a flash of black light, and Levi swore as the blue light singed his damaged eyes.

But then Rohan's sword seemed to draw in the light that surrounded them, casting the room into enough darkness for Levi to be able to see. Rohan dragged his sword across his hand, and then Levi called out his own axe and did the same. The warriors clasped hands, and Levi felt energy surge through him as Rohan's magic became a part of him. He felt the instant bond with this ancient warrior, and centuries of hardship and anguish flooded him. His gaze shot to Rohan, shocked by the depth of the warrior's torment. It was a thousand times the weight that Levi had ever carried. How could the man stay sane under so much weight?

Rohan's voice filled his mind. *Warrior to warrior. Bound by blood. Connected across all distances. Sworn to defend and fight side by side, at all costs. So be it.*

Levi didn't hesitate. *Warrior to warrior. Bound by blood. Connected across all distances. Sworn to defend and fight side by side, at all costs. So be it.* Power surged through him, and he felt his soul reach out and connect to Rohan's. It was different from the blood bond with Maya, but at the same time, it was the same. Extraordinarily powerful, a steadfast connection he knew would hold across all distances, one that went both ways. He realized that not only had he sworn fealty to Rohan, but that Rohan had sworn the same fealty to him.

Rohan then knelt down and carved an outline in the dirt, in the shape of Levi's weapon. He backed up and went down on one knee, gesturing for Levi to position himself by the drawing he'd etched in the dirt. "I will summon my team, and the induction will be complete."

Levi's throat tightened at the sight of the empty spot. That was his spot. He was going to become a part of a group, a team, a family of damn heroes whose job it was to save the world. As he stood there, six warriors strode into the cavern in single file. They were all wearing cloaks and their hoods were up. They walked into the cavern, forming a semi-circle with the empty spot at the top of it. "The shadows have been vanquished," one of them said. "It's over."

Maya sagged in relief, and he pulled her against him, pressing a kiss to the top of her head. *You did it, sweetheart.*

She looked up at him. *We did it. Together.* There was so much warmth in her eyes that he felt his heart swell in response.

Not a bad team, eh?

You're about to get more teammates. She nodded toward the other warriors, and he looked back as they took up positions, forming a circle with two openings. There was one open space where his weapon had been carved into the ground, and another open spot by Rohan's right side, where he assumed Thano would be when he returned.

As one, they went down on their left knees and called their weapons out in their right hands. Each warrior extended it upward, toward the heavens in silent homage. "Take your rightful place, warrior," Rohan said.

Levi hesitated. Was he really worthy to call himself a hero? He was one of the bad guys, a black scourge on humanity—

Shut up, Levi. You're gifted, you're loved, and you're worthy. So get up there, and claim your destiny, the one you actually deserve. Maya's fingers wrapped around his, and his tension eased at the feel of her hand in his.

He grinned down at her. *I love you.*

She smiled back. *I know. You can ravage me later, but the boys are waiting. Come on.* She tugged lightly on his hand, and then led him through the center of the circle to his spot at the top. Once he took his position, she started to back away, but he put his arm over her shoulder, holding her there. *I can't do this without you. Stay with me.*

She moved beside him, tucking herself against his side. Her hand rested on his waist, and he felt himself relax. With Maya by his side, he knew he could become the man that Rohan believed he was.

Silence fell over the room as they waited, and then, finally, Levi heard the steady clip-clop of Thano's horse as the warrior returned. Levi glanced toward the door as Apollo strode in. But Thano wasn't alone. He was holding a woman in front of him on the saddle. She was pale and thin, leaning heavily on Thano, held upright only by his strength.

Maya glanced over, and then sucked in her breath. "Elisabeth?" Her voice broke as the woman's head turned toward Maya.

Her eyes were a deep blue, exactly like Maya's, and Levi knew then that it was her sister, reclaimed from the shadows by Merk's sunlight. "Maya?"

"Oh, God." Maya held up her arms as Thano gently lowered Elisabeth into them. Levi helped support Elisabeth as she fell against her sister, the two women clinging desperately to each other. Tears streamed down Maya's cheeks, and Levi's chest tightened. So much love. How had he missed out on this part of life for so long? He still couldn't believe that this was his life, that a woman who poured out so much love was his.

"You saved us, little sister," Elisabeth said, pulling back so she could look at Maya. "This is your kingdom. I'll step aside for you. We need you."

Maya looked up at Levi, and he saw the joy gleaming in her eyes. She'd gotten everything she wanted. But then, to her surprise, she shook her head. "I don't have time to run a kingdom anymore, Elisabeth." She reached out, entwining her finger through Levi's. "I'm part of another team now, and I'm the only one who can do it. It's your birthright. They need you."

Levi's throat tightened at her words, and he gently turned her toward him. "Maya, this is what you've always wanted."

She shook her head. "I wanted to matter, Levi. That's what I wanted. And I realized I do. I don't need to be the queen. You taught me that, and Merk taught me how stupid I was to worry about all that stuff." She looped her arms around her sister's shoulders. "You're the one who needs to lead this kingdom. I don't need it."

Her sister's blue eyes lit with warmth, and Levi knew then that Maya had always been loved. She'd just had to realize it. "Are you sure?"

Maya nodded, holding up their clasped hands. "This is where I belong. With him. He makes me better."

Levi kissed the top of her head. "She makes me whole."

Elisabeth smiled, a smile that lit up her tired eyes. "I love you, Maya. Thank you for not giving up this battle."

"I love you too, sis." The women hugged again, and Levi grinned, unable to keep the smile off his face. She'd been given the kingdom, but she'd chosen *him*.

"I need to sit." Elisabeth sank down on a nearby rock. "Can I watch?"

Rohan nodded, and she smiled, hugging her knees to her chest as if she couldn't keep herself warm. Thano tossed her his jacket, and she wrapped it around her shoulders, shooting him a grateful smile before turning her gaze to her sister. "I'm so proud of you, Maya."

Maya grinned and looked up at Levi. "Team effort."

"Yeah, it is." He wrapped his arm around her. "I'd stay here and help you with your kingdom, you know. You don't need to turn it down." He needed her to understand that. His love wasn't conditional.

"I know. I want to go with you." She met his gaze. "I spent my life living in the shadows of this kingdom, and now it's time for me to really live. With you."

He nodded. "Always with me." Their fingers intertwined, Levi turned back toward the circle, to the waiting ring of warriors. A feeling of rightness settled deep within him as he looked around the cavern at the men who had dedicated their lives to a mission greater than them. There was a time not so long ago when he'd thought it was crap to belong to a greater cause, but that was when he'd thought it wasn't within reach. But now?

He wanted to be that guy, and he wanted to do it with the woman who had saved his soul. "I'm ready."

Rohan nodded, and his deep voice rang out. "We shall begin."

Sneak Peek: Dark Wolf Rising

A *Heart of the Shifter* Novel

Bryn McKenzie would be dead by Thursday.

And it was going to be an ugly, terrible death.

It was almost two in the morning, she hadn't slept yet, and she knew she wouldn't. She just waited in the bed in the hotel room, staring at the ceiling, listening to the low conversation of the men in her living room.

Men who had been assigned to protect her.

Men who would fail.

They thought they knew how to keep her safe, but they hadn't seen what she had seen...which was why she had to die. No one who'd witnessed that particular murder would be allowed to live, and she knew that.

She'd known it when she'd gone to the police and told them what had happened.

She'd known it when she'd agreed to testify at Jace Donovan's trial.

She'd known it when her team of highly skilled police officers had set her up in this hotel room, determined to keep her alive long enough to testify.

And yet she'd done all of it anyway, and she would stay here and hope she was wrong, because a woman had died in front of her, and Bryn was the only one who knew who had done it. There was no way she could stay silent when the man who'd killed that innocent woman went free.

She was trying to do the right thing for once in her life. After her mom had died when she was seventeen, the guilt had driven Bryn into a self-destructive hell to hide from the pain. She'd been fighting her way back ever since, but she still felt like the shadows of the accident and the subsequent dark time in her life were always haunting her. If she died trying to bring justice to the monster who'd slaughtered an innocent woman, then at least she'd die trying to do something worthy with her life. But she didn't want to die yet, not until she'd made sure that the man who'd killed Kate Stephens paid for his crime. It wasn't enough to want to make a difference. She had to actually make it. If she could stay alive long enough to testify, then maybe she could begin to understand why she'd survived the car accident that had killed her mother.

She knew she might be assassinated before the trial, and she'd accepted that risk, but God help her, she didn't *want* to die, and she really didn't want to die the way Kate had died: slowly, agonizingly in a pool of her own blood, with her throat ripped from her body.

Bryn squeezed her eyes shut against the images that wouldn't leave her mind, the image of that horrible moment, that brutal attack, the screams that hadn't stopped ringing through her mind since it had happened. "Breathe, Bryn," she whispered, trying to slow the sudden racing of her heart. "It's okay. Right now, you're perfectly safe. No one has hunted you down yet—"

She suddenly became aware that the living room had gone silent. The men had stopped talking.

Her heart leapt into her throat, and she bolted upright in bed. Was this it? Was it happening now? She leapt to her feet, grabbed the gun with the silver bullets from her nightstand, and backed into the corner, aiming at the door of the bedroom. She'd already dragged the heavy hotel dresser and couch in front of the door, but she knew it wouldn't save her. Her hands were shaking, and sweat was pouring down her back. Dear God. How had they found her?

There was a low growl from the living room, and she froze, fear paralyzing her. *Dear God. A wolf.* Then one of the men screamed, and a frenzy of growls and snarls erupted from the living room. Gunshots. Crashes. Howls. Screams.

Dear God. The men were being murdered.

She looked down at the gun in her hands, and she grimaced at the sight of her shaking fingers wrapped around the metal. Trained, armed men were being slaughtered out there, and she thought a gun would help her? She had to get out, to run while she had time. Frantic, she raced to the window. She was on the fifth floor. Too high to jump. Another crash sounded from the living room, and more gunshots.

There had to be handholds. She wasn't going to die

tonight, and she wasn't going to die the way Kate had, slaughtered by a werewolf. She shoved the gun into the waistband of her jeans and reached for the window—

A hand clamped down over her mouth and someone dragged her backward, away from the window.

A silent scream erupted from her throat, and she fought frantically, desperate, but whoever held her was a thousand times stronger than her. God, no, she wasn't ready to die—

"It's a rose," her captor whispered into her ear. "A white rose for friendship, a red rose for your heart, and a blue rose because the impossible is always possible."

She froze in disbelief. She hadn't heard that poem since she was fourteen, and wildly in love with her best friend, Cash Burns, who had disappeared without explanation one dark night. It couldn't be him. She hadn't heard from him or found any trace of his existence in thirteen years.

"It's me, Bryn," he said. "Don't make a sound."

Tears filled her eyes as she recognized his voice, a voice she'd never thought she'd hear again. Why was Cash in her room? How was he here? She nodded once, and he immediately released his death grip on her mouth.

She spun around, and her heart seemed to stop at the sight of him. She remembered a thin, gawky fifteen year old, but standing before her, illuminated by the moonlight, was a heavily muscled man with piercing green eyes so intense they seemed to bore right through her. His hair was dark and long, ragged. His black T-shirt stretched across his muscled chest, and several long-healed scars crisscrossed his left temple. He was pure danger, elemental male, and wildly sensual, a man she never would have recognized as her childhood friend. "Cash?"

Another shout echoed from the living room, jerking her attention to the door. The door was closed, but the dresser and couch were ajar, showing how Cash had gotten into the room. Clearly, the heavy furniture had been nothing to him, with his strong frame.

"It's my job to kill you. We have to make it look good." He pulled out a heavy knife. "Scream like I'm ripping you up." Then he dragged the knife across his forearm, spilling blood all over the carpet. "Scream. Now."

She screamed, a scream that tore from her throat and never seemed to stop. Cash was bleeding all over the carpet, taking the injury to his arm without even flinching. Good God. Who had he become? She backed away as he dragged the comforter off the bed.

"Lie down on it," he ordered. "I'll wrap you up when I take you out through there, and they won't know you're still alive. But we have to move fast. They'll be in here in seconds."

She gaped at him, a million scenarios rushing through her head. The door of the bedroom shook as something flew into it. There were fewer human screams now, and more growling and howling. "You're with them? With the werewolves? How?"

His eyes glittered. "Now, Bryn, or I can't save you." His voice was low and urgent. "They have to think you're dead."

She understood suddenly why he'd cut himself. The wolves needed to smell blood on the comforter. "Won't they know it's your blood?"

"Yeah, but they're distracted. It should be enough. Now."

She had a split second to decide whether to trust him, a man she hadn't seen in over a decade, who was now, apparently, killing people for a pack of werewolves. He was a stranger, but he was also Cash, and he was her only chance. She'd believed in him once. She had to pray that his heart hadn't changed the way his body had. "Give me the knife."

He handed it to her without question, and she dragged it across her own forearm. He swore as she cut herself, leaping toward her and yanking the knife out of her hand. "What the hell was that for?"

"It had to be my blood. They'll know." Her knees buckled and her head spun as the pain hit. She bit her lip, fighting back gasps of pain as she cradled her arm to her chest.

He caught her, his hands framing her waist as her knees started to give out. "Shit, Bryn. You haven't changed at all." But his voice was affectionate as he helped her down to the floor. "I missed you, babe."

"You didn't miss me. You ditched me, vanished from my life without a word." She stretched out on the floor, yelping when her injured arm brushed against her knee.

"I missed you," he repeated, his voice softer this time. Their eyes met, and she saw in them the person she'd once known, who she'd trusted with her life so many times before.

She nodded once, then lay down. "If you get me killed, I'll never forgive you."

"A threat that still works with me." He winked at her, then paused just long enough to trace his fingers across her cheeks. "Bryn," he said softly, his touch achingly familiar, and yet, so different from what it had once been.

A wolf howled in the living room, and he swore. "See you on the flip side, babe."

She nodded. "Okay." She kept eye contact with him as long as she could, and she didn't miss the flash of regret across his face before he flipped the blanket over her.

She sucked in her breath and rolled over, letting him truss her up in the stuffy fabric. Her arms were trapped against her sides, and her legs were locked together, entombing her in the comforter. She was utterly defenseless. Panic hit her, and she started to struggle, unable to stop herself.

"Bryn." His voice as a low whisper, and she felt him touch her shoulder through the comforter. "It's just like when we were kids. Be dead."

She squeezed her eyes shut. "Just how good are you?" she asked. "There are wolves out there! What if they come after me?"

"I'm a serious, fucking badass, babe. I'm a thousand times what I was as a kid. I'll keep you alive, I swear." His voice radiated cocky arrogance, just like it had when they were teens, only now his voice was deep, sliding over her skin like a sensual caress.

Heat flushed her body, and she thought back to the number of times that he'd stepped up and taken the heat for her, the way the bullies in the school always left him alone, terrified of the raw strength and power in his thin frame. Back then, he'd been the badass that no one expected, and now, he was pure muscle and man, apparently on the payroll of a pack of wolves. Which would trump, his loyalty to the pack, or to her? "What if you have to kill them to keep me alive?"

He paused for a long moment. "Then I'll kill them."

She felt the truth in his voice, and tears filled her eyes. God, it had been so long since anyone had stood up for her the way he always had. She hadn't realized how much she'd missed that feeling of knowing that she didn't have to fight her battles on her own. "Damn you," she said softly.

He laughed quietly, squeezing her ass through the comforter, a move that had been obnoxious when they were teens, but that now sent heat cascading through her. "I love it when I make you cry. You ready?"

She knew he wasn't asking if she was ready. He was asking if she trusted him. She let out a deep breath, and spoke the truth. Cash had always been the one she believed in, and she still did, despite the gaping emptiness of time since she'd last seen him. "Yes. Let's go."

"That's my girl." He scooped her up and slung her over his shoulder, his arm locking her down against him as he headed for the door that separated them from the wolves that had been sent to kill her.

Sneak Peek: Leopard's Kiss

A *Shadow Guardian* Novel

Anya Diaz felt as if invisible fingers were sliding down her spine in a sensual caress of lethal danger. Fear rippled through her, and for a brief second, she wondered if meeting this unknown contact was worth the risk. She couldn't afford a single mistake, and she really couldn't afford to die.

She swallowed, her mouth dry, wishing she'd ordered water instead of tequila that she'd never drink.

She feigned a look across the room, slanting a sideways glance behind her, trying to ascertain the cause of the sensation along her spine. Her breath caught when she saw a man, well over six feet, wearing a black leather trench coat, standing several yards behind her, his gaze boring into her. His dark hair was short, his blue eyes so intense it was as if they were made of pure fire. Even through his coat, she could tell he was heavily muscled, a predator more than a man. He was unshaven, his dark whiskers making shadows fall across his angular cheeks. He looked like he lived in untamed wilds beyond the reaches of civilization, a man who lived by his own rules, not the ones society tried to impress upon him. He was pure sex, deadly sin, and unmitigated danger…and he was staring at her.

Her heartrate began to escalate as his gaze dropped to her mouth, his eyes darkening as if he were imagining what she tasted like, what she would feel like against him. Desire pooled in her belly, desire that was completely out of character for her. She'd learned her lesson long ago about letting her need for a man rule her, and she never bothered to notice men anymore… but it was impossible for her to drag her gaze off him.

She felt as though his hands were gliding over her skin, touching every inch of her body as he assessed her. She shivered, trying to shake off the desire pulsing low in her belly, the need he was awakening in her, even though she'd never seen him before in her life.

He was clearly there for one reason, and that reason was her.

Except he wasn't the person she'd come there to meet. He was all wrong…but she couldn't stop her response to him.

He walked toward her, moving with the lithe grace of a predator. As he got closer, a cold chill seemed to wrap around her, the chill of death, and danger. She stiffened, sliding her hand along her lower back for the dagger she'd hidden beneath her shirt. It was small, but she was very good with it. She'd known how to defend herself since she was three, but as he neared, doubt flickered through her. He radiated raw power, the kind that could devastate his prey without him so much as blinking.

He was a man who delivered death, she was sure of it. Her heartrate sped up as he neared, and a cold sweat broke out between her shoulder blades. She didn't know if she could defeat him, and she didn't have time to try. *Keep walking*, she urged him silently. *Just keep walking.*

One dark eyebrow quirked at her, and for a split second, she thought he'd heard her silent command. Then his gaze dropped to her mouth again, sending searing heat cascading through her. She caught her breath, as he raised his gaze to hers again. His expression didn't change, and his stride didn't falter as he walked right past her toward the bar.

She let her breath out, her hands shaking with relief as she wiped her wrist across her damp brow. The intensity of her response to him was shocking. What was going on?

He took over a seat at the bar, still staring at her. Her moment of relief fled, replaced by rising tension. He wasn't even trying to hide the way he was watching her. His gaze was locked on her, watching and assessing her every move. The way he'd eased onto the edge of the bar stool, relaxed yet primed to react in a split second, made him look like a wild panther, a predator so agile and lethal that he could take her out in a single leap. He was too dangerous to be handsome, and too elusive to be appealing, and yet, there was something about him that was drawing her in. Something compelling. Something…

Yes. You want me.

A deep, darkly seductive male voice rolled through her mind, making her belly clench with desire. Had he just spoken in her *mind*? The voice was sensual, rough, erotic, with a hint of accented culture that made her think of black tie dinners and foreign royalty instead of the dangerous predator sitting so still on his perch.

Don't hold back. His voice slid through her mind again, a sensual caress that made her belly tighten with desire. *Think about kissing me. Think about my hands sliding over your naked skin—*

"Stop it." She glared fiercely at him. The satisfied gleam in his eyes told her that it *was* him in her head. "I didn't invite you in there. Get out."

He didn't smile, and he didn't back off. *What's your darkest fantasy? Handcuffs? A threesome? A little pain...* As he spoke, images of each scenario flashed through her mind. Her naked, silken ties around her wrists—

"No." She jerked her gaze away from him, breaking the connection. She fisted her hands, quickly weaving safeguards in her mind, invisible walls that encased every last thought, every feeling, every bit of herself that wasn't physical. Within a millisecond, he was out of her mind. Her lungs expanded in a sudden relief as the sensual sensation of being caressed along her spine vanished. Had it been *his* touch she'd been feeling on her back? Some metaphysical extension of his mind that felt like a real caress and seduction? What kind of power did he carry? And why was he directing it at her?

His expression didn't change, but he seemed to become even more still.

She met his gaze, daring him to try again.

He did.

She felt him testing her protections, feeling his way through her mind, searching for the one gap she'd missed. Anya smiled, allowing the same satisfied gleam into her eyes that he'd had in his. "I'm good," she said. "Don't bother."

He didn't answer, his gaze flicking behind her.

She sensed the approach at the same moment, and she sat up more erectly in sudden anticipation, sensing that the person approaching her from behind was the one she'd come to meet. Her instructions had been not to turn around, and not to look, or the deal would be off. Someone leaned up against her seat, and a warm breath brushed over her neck.

Anya's heart began to pound. This was it. Her chance.

"Is Julia still alive?" she asked, her breath frozen in her chest as she waited for news of her best friend, her only friend, the only person still alive who mattered to her.

Fingers drifted through her hair, and lips brushed over the back of her neck. A seduction, for anyone in the bar who was bothering to watch. A charade to protect them both. "For now." It was a woman's voice, breathy and sensual.

Tears of relief burned in Anya's eyes. Alive. Her best friend was *alive*. "How do I find her?" She slid her gaze toward the mirror behind the bar, taking a forbidden look at the woman she'd spent the last three weeks hunting down. Raven black, ultra-straight hair reached just past her shoulders, and her eyes were hidden behind dark glasses. Her lips were pale, her skin the color of a latte, and her simple outfit of a tight black tank top and fitted jeans made her look sexy, but unmemorable. Who was she? How did she know what had happened to Julia? How was she involved? She'd found the woman's email address in Julia's belongings, the only clue she had as to what had happened to her friend. It had taken weeks to track this woman down, and longer to convince her to meet…assuming the woman standing behind her was the same person who had answered her emails.

The man at the bar leaned forward, drawing Anya's attention off the mirror and back to him. He was staring at her even more intensely, his gaze boring into hers as if it were a dagger that could cut out her heart. She could feel him testing her psychic defenses, trying to get back in her mind.

She jerked her gaze off him, refusing to let him distract her. She closed her eyes to cut him off, so she could focus on the woman behind her. She couldn't afford to miss a word. "Where is Julia?"

The woman's breath tickled her neck. "You must go to the warehouse on the corner of Hartford and—"

Fingers closed around her wrist. Anya's eyes snapped open as she was jerked off her feet and across the floor. She slammed into the hard body of the man at the bar, and his arms locked around her. He stared down into her eyes. No longer were his eyes blue. They had shifted into dark, bottomless pits of death…and something else. Something more dangerous. Something more personal.

"I love you," he said, his whisper rolling through her, making sudden tears fill her eyes as longing swept over her. To be loved, to be held like she mattered, to be—

He kissed her.

Not just a kiss.

A kiss so tender, so beautiful, so seductive that it made her heart cry for more. Never had she been kissed like that. *Ever.* His lips were decadently soft, his tongue a sensual dance of promise and tenderness, his hands on her hips like he was her shield against the world. He was pure male, offering himself to her as her protector, her lover, the man who would never let her be alone again.

Her soul cried out for his kiss and his declarations with an intensity so strong that it made her heart ache with longing. The pain jerked her back into her own mind just enough for her to realize that something was wrong, terribly wrong. He was in her mind again, reeling her in, offering her the words and emotions that she burned for, as if he knew exactly what triggers would ensnare her. He was manipulating her, drawing her into his kiss…with a sinking heart, she realized suddenly that his kiss was his weapon, wielded with the skillful, ruthless finesse of a well-practiced assassin Why had he come for her? Sudden fear pulsed through her, and she knew it had to be because of Julia. Was he trying to keep her from talking to the woman? Or was he there to kill her?

She was in danger. Sudden, dire danger from him. She had to break his hold on her. She had to talk to the woman. She had to find Julia. She shoved at his chest, trying to raise her mental shields and boot him out of her mind—

He deepened the kiss, a searing hot kiss that seemed to ignite her very soul. His lips were hot and sensual, his kiss deep and intoxicating, sending desire sparking through every part of her body. Yearning filled her, a desperate need for him, for his kiss, for his touch, for everything he could offer her.

In the deep recesses of her mind, she knew it was wrong. She knew what she felt was unnatural, but the realization was faint, fading, too weak for her to grasp. He tunneled his hands through her hair, angling her head as he deepened the kiss, drawing her away from her mission and into his spell.

She couldn't stop herself from responding to his seduction. Her soul was crying out for him. She could sense the danger he presented. She could feel the emptiness of his soul. She knew that his whispers of love were lies he didn't mean. But it didn't matter. Something about him called to her, something far deeper than the seduction he was weaving in her mind.

She needed to stab him.

She needed to run.

But she couldn't.

She simply wanted *him.*

Sneak Peek: A Real Cowboy Rides a Motorcycle

A *Wyoming Rebels* Novel

He was tired.

He was cranky.

He was wet.

Zane Stockton idled his motorcycle outside his brother's ranch house, narrowing his eyes at the darkened windows. Gone was the time when he'd let himself in and crash. There was a woman in there now, and that changed all the rules, especially when it was two in the morning.

He probably shouldn't have come tonight, but he was here, and he was done being on the road for now. Rain had been thundering down on him for hours, and he was drenched all the way to his bones. He just wanted to sleep and forget about all the crap that had gone down today.

Trying not to rev the engine too much, he eased his bike down the driveway past the barn and turned right into the lean-to beside the bunkhouse. He settled his bike and whipped out a couple towels to clean it off, making sure it was mud-free before calling it a night.

He grabbed his bag from the back of the bike, scowling when he realized it had gotten wet, then sloshed across the puddles toward the front door of the bunkhouse. He retrieved the key from the doorframe, and pried the thing open.

It was pitch dark inside, but he knew his way around and didn't bother with a light. He dropped the bag, kicked off his boots and his drenched clothes, then headed for the only bed that was still set up in the place, ever since Steen and Erin had rearranged it for their own use during their temporary stay there. At least they'd upgraded their lodging so the bunkhouse was now available again for use by the family vagrant.

Zane jerked back the covers and collapsed onto the bed. The minute he landed, he felt the soft, very real feel of a body beneath him, including the swell of a woman's breast beneath his forearm. Shit! "What the hell?" He leapt to his feet just as a woman shrieked and slammed a pillow into the side of his head.

"Hey, I'm not going to hurt you! I'm Chase's brother!" He grabbed the pillow as it clocked him in the side of the head again. "Stop!"

There was a moment of silence, and all he could hear was heavy breathing. Then she spoke. "You're Chase's brother?" Her voice was breathless, and throaty, as if he'd awakened her out of a deep sleep, which he probably had. It sounded sexy as hell, and he was shocked to feel a rush of desire catapult through him.

Shit. He hadn't responded physically to a woman in a long time, and now he'd run into a woman who could turn him on simply by *speaking* to him? Who the hell was she? "Yeah," he said, sounding crankier than he intended. "Who are you?"

"You're Steen?" He heard her fumbling for something, and he wondered if she was searching for a baseball bat, pepper spray, or something that indicated she hadn't been nearly as turned on by his voice as he'd been by hers.

"No, a different brother," he replied, his head spinning as he tried to figure what was going on, and why he was reacting to her so intensely. "I'm Zane. Harmless. Good guy. No need to decapitate me."

There was a pause in her movements. "I wasn't going to decapitate you. I was looking for my shirt."

"Your shirt?" he echoed blankly. "You're not wearing a shirt?" He hadn't noticed much bare skin for that brief moment he'd been on top of her. How had he missed it?

"I'm wearing a camisole, but it's not exactly decent. Give me a sec." A small laugh drifted through the darkness. "You're such a guy. Of course you'd fixate on the possibility of me being naked. Do all men think only of sex?"

He grinned, relaxing. He'd startled her, but she'd regrouped quickly, and he liked that. She wasn't a wimp who was running to the door screaming. "What's your name?" he asked.

"Taylor Shaw. I'm Mira's best friend from home. I surprised her for a visit, but it turns out, there's no space in the house."

"Nope. Not anymore. I'm displaced too." He suddenly wanted to see her. "You decent yet?"

"Yes, but barely—"

He reached over and flicked on the small light by the bed. The soft yellow glow was less harsh than the overhead light, but it still took his eyes a moment to adjust to the brightness. When they did, he saw Taylor sitting on the bed, curly blond hair tumbling around her shoulders in a disheveled mess that made her look completely adorable. Her eyes were green, fixed on him as she squinted against the sudden light. He could see the curve of her shoulders beneath the light pink, long-sleeved shirt she was wearing. The faint outline of a white camisole was evident beneath her shirt, not quite obscuring the fact that she wasn't wearing a bra. Her gray yoga pants were frayed at the knee and cuff, but they fit her hips with perfection. She looked like she'd just tumbled right out of a bed, and she was sexy as hell.

But it was her face that caught his attention. Her gaze was wary, but there was a vulnerability in it that made him want to protect her. He had zero protective instincts when it came to women…until now, until he'd met this woman who'd tried to defend herself with a pillow.

Then her gaze slid down his body, and his entire body went into heated overdrive. It wasn't until her eyes widened in horror when her gaze was at hip level that he remembered something very important.

He was naked.

Sneak Peek: Prince Charming Can Wait

An *Ever After* Novel

Clouds were thick in the sky, blocking the moon. The lake and the woods were dark, swallowing up light and life, like a soothing blanket of nothingness coating the night. Emma needed to get away from the world she didn't belong to, the one that held no place for her. Tears were thick in her throat, her eyes stinging as she ran. The stones were wet from the rain earlier in the day, and the cool dampness sent chills through her.

She reached the dock and leapt out onto the damp wood. Her foot slipped, and she yelped as she lost her balance—

Strong hands shot out and grabbed her around the waist, catching her before she fell into the water. Shrieking in surprise, she jerked free, twisting out of range. The evasive move sent her off balance again, her feet went out from under her, and she was falling—

And again, someone grabbed her. "Hey," a low voice said. "I'm not going to hurt you."

Emma froze at the sound of the voice she knew so well, the one that had haunted her for so many sleepless nights. The voice she thought she'd never hear again, because he'd been gone for so long. "Harlan?"

"Yeah."

Emma spun around in his grasp, and her breath caught as she saw his shadowed face. His eyes were dark and hooded in the filtered light, his cheek bones more prominent than they had been the last time she'd seen him. Heavy stubble framed his face, and his hair was long and ragged around the base of his neck. He was leaner than she remembered, but his muscles were more defined, straining at his tee shirt. He looked grungy and real, a man who lived by the earth every day of his life. He exuded pure strength and raw appeal that ignited something deep within her. She instinctively leaned toward him, into the strength that emanated from him. His hands felt hot and dangerous where they clasped her hips, but she had no urge to push him away.

Damn him. After not seeing him for nearly a year, he

still affected her beyond reason.

"You're back," she managed.

"Yeah."

Again, the one word answer. He had never said much more than that to her, but she'd seen him watching her intently on countless occasions, his piercing blue eyes roiling with so much unspoken emotion and turbulence. She managed a small smile, trying to hide the intensity of her reaction to seeing him. "Astrid didn't mention you would be here."

"She doesn't know." Again, he fell silent, but he raised one hand and lifted a lock of her hair, thumbing it gently. "Like silk," he said softly. "Just as I always thought it would feel."

Her heart began to pound now. There was no way to stop it, not when she was so close to him, not when she could feel his hands on her, a touch she'd craved since the first time she'd seen him. It had been two years ago, the day she'd walked back into her life in Birch Crossing. He had been leaning against the deli counter in Wright's, his arms folded over his chest, his piercing blue eyes watching her so intently.

And now he was here, in these woods, holding onto her.

His grip was strong, but his touch was gentle in her hair as he filtered the strands through his fingers. "You've thought about my hair before?" she asked. Ridiculous question, but it tumbled out anyway. And she wanted to know. Had he really thought about her before? Was she not alone in the way her mind had wandered to him so many nights when she hadn't been able to sleep?

His gaze met hers, and for a second, heat seemed to explode between them. Then he dropped his hands and stepped back. The loss of his touch was like ice cold water drenching her, and she had to hug herself to keep from reaching out for him.

"Tell Astrid I was here," he said. "I'm leaving again—"

"What?" She couldn't hold back the protest. "Already? Why?"

"I have a job."

That job. That mysterious job. He had never told Astrid, or anyone else in town, where he went when he disappeared. Sometimes, he was in town for months, playing at his real estate business, taking off for only a few days at a time. Other times, he was absent for longer. This last time, he'd been gone for almost a year, which was the longest that anyone could remember him being away. And he was leaving again already? "Astrid misses you," Emma said quickly, instinctively trying to give him a reason not to disappear again. "You can't leave without at least saying hi."

Harlan's gaze flickered to the house, and his mouth tightened. He made no move to join the celebration, and suddenly she realized that he felt the same way she did about invading that happy little world. He didn't belong to it any more than she did. Empathy tightened her chest, and she looked more carefully at the independent man who no one in town had ever been able to get close to. "You can stop by and see her tomorrow," she said softly.

He didn't move, and he didn't take his eyes off the house. "She's happy? Jason's good to her?"

Emma nodded. "He treasures her. They're so in love." She couldn't quite keep the ache out of her voice, and she saw Harlan look sharply at her.

"What's wrong?" he asked. "Why did you say it like that?"

"No, no, they're great. Really." She swallowed and pulled back her shoulders, refusing to let herself yearn for that which she did not want or need in her life. "She would kill me if she found out I let you leave town without seeing her. How long until you have to go?"

He shifted. "Forty-eight hours." The confession was reluctant.

"So, then, come back here tomorrow and see her," she said, relief rushing through her at the idea that he wasn't leaving town immediately. For at least two nights, she could sleep knowing that he was breathing the same air as she was.

"No, not here." He ran his hand through his hair, and she saw a dark bruise on the underside of his triceps. "You guys still go to Wright's in the morning for coffee?"

Emma's heart fluttered at his question. For a man who had held himself aloof, he seemed endearingly aware of what his sister did every day...and he knew that she was always there as well. "Yes. We'll be there at eight thirty."

He nodded. "Yeah, okay, I'll try to make it then." He glanced at her again, and just like before, heat seemed to rush through her—

Then he turned away, stealing that warmth from her before she'd had time to finish savoring it. "No." She grabbed his arm, her fingers sliding over his hard muscles. Shocked by the feel of his body beneath her palm, she jerked back, but not soon enough.

He froze under her touch, sucking in his breath. Slowly, he turned his head to look back at her. "No?"

"Don't *try* to make it tomorrow morning," she said quickly, trying to pretend her panic had been on Astrid's behalf, not her own. "You *have* to make it. Astrid needs to see you. She wants you to meet Rosie. She's happy, Harlan, but she needs her brother, too. Jason is her family, but so are you, and you know how she needs to be connected."

Harlan closed his eyes for a long moment, and she saw emotions warring within him. For a man so stoic and aloof, he was fermenting with emotions in a way that she'd never seen before. She looked again at the bruise on his arm. "Are you okay, Harlan? What happened while you were gone?" There was no way to keep the concern out of her voice, no way to hide that her heart ached at the thought of him being hurt.

His eyes opened again. He said nothing, but he suddenly wrapped his hand around the back of her neck.

She stiffened, her heart pounding as he drew her close to him. "What are you doing?"

"I need this." Then he captured her mouth with his.

She had no time to be afraid, no time to fear. His kiss was too desperate for her to be afraid. It wasn't a kiss to seduce or dominate. It was a burning, aching need for connection, for humanity, for something to chase away the darkness hunting him...everything she needed in a kiss as well.

Her hands went instinctively to his chest, bracing, protecting, but at the same time, connecting. She kissed him back, needing the same touch that he did, desperate for that feeling of being wanted. She didn't know this man, and yet, on some level, she'd known him for so long. She'd seen his torment, she'd felt his isolation, and she'd witnessed his unfailing need to protect Astrid, even if he had never inserted himself fully into her life.

Somehow, Harlan's kiss wasn't a threat the way other men's were. He was leaving town, so he was no more than a shadow that would ease into her life and then disappear. He wouldn't try to take her, to trick her, to consume her. He wouldn't make promises and then betray them. All he wanted was the same thing she did, a break from the isolation that locked him down, a fragile whisper of human connection to fill the gaping hole in his heart.

"Emma!" Astrid's voice rang out in the night, shattering the moment. "Are you out here?"

Harlan broke the kiss, but he didn't move away, keeping his lips against hers. One of his hands was tangled lightly in her hair, the other was locked around her waist. Somehow, he'd pulled them close, until her breasts were against his chest, their bodies melted together. It felt so right, but at the same time, a familiar anxiety began to build inside Emma at the intimacy.

"Do not fear me, sweet Emma," Harlan whispered against her lips. "I would only treasure what you give."

His voice was so soft and tender that her throat tightened. How she'd yearned for so many years, for a lifetime, for someone to speak to her like that...until she'd finally become smart enough to relinquish that dream. And now, here it was, in the form of a man who would disappear from her life in forty-eight hours, maybe never to return. Which was why it was okay, because she didn't have to worry that he would want more than she could give, or that she would give him more than she could afford. Maybe she didn't belong in the room of couples and families, but for this brief moment, she belonged out in the night, with a man who lived the same existence that she did.

"Emma?" Astrid's footsteps sounded on the deck, and Harlan released her.

"Don't tell her I was here," he said. "I'll come by Wright's in the morning. Now is not the time." Then, without a sound, he faded into the darkness, vanishing so quickly she almost wondered whether she'd imagined him.

Select List of Other Books by Stephanie Rowe

(For a complete book list, please visit www.stephanierowe.com)

PARANORMAL ROMANCE

The *Heart of the Shifter* Series

Dark Wolf Rising
12/15/15

The *Shadow Guardian* Series

Leopard's Kiss
Early 2016

The *NightHunter* Series

Not Quite Dead

The *Order of the Blade* Series

Darkness Awakened
Darkness Seduced
Darkness Surrendered
Forever in Darkness
Darkness Reborn
Darkness Arisen
Darkness Unleashed
Inferno of Darkness
Darkness Possessed
Shadows of Darkness
Hunt the Darkness
2016
Order of the Blade Box Set Books 1 - 3

The *Soulfire* Series

Kiss at Your Own Risk
Touch if You Dare
Hold Me if You Can

The *Immortally Sexy* Series

Date Me Baby, One More Time
Must Love Dragons
He Loves Me, He Loves Me Hot
Sex & the Immortal Bad Boy

ROMANTIC SUSPENSE

The *Alaska Heat* Series

Ice
Chill
Ghost

CONTEMPORARY ROMANCE

The *Wyoming Rebels* Series

A Real Cowboy Never Says No
A Real Cowboy Knows How to Kiss
A Real Cowboy Rides a Motorcyc;e

The *Ever After* Series

No Knight Needed
Fairy Tale Not Required
Prince Charming Can Wait

Stand Alone Novels

Jingle This!

NONFICTION

Essays

The Feel Good Life

FOR TEENS

The *A Girlfriend's Guide to Boys* Series

Putting Boys on the Ledge
Studying Boys

Who Needs Boys?
Smart Boys & Fast Girls

Stand Alone Novels

The Fake Boyfriend Experiment

FOR PRE-TEENS

The *Forgotten* Series

Penelope Moonswoggle, The Girl Who Could Not Ride a Dragon
Penelope Moonswoggle & the Accidental Doppelganger
Release Date TBD

Collections

Box Sets

Alpha Immortals
Alphas Unwrapped
12/1/15
Last Hero Standing
Mischief Under the Mistletoe
11/17/15
Wicked After Dark
10/6/15

Stephanie Rowe Bio

New York Times and *USA Today* bestselling author Stephanie Rowe is the author of more than 40 novels, including her popular Order of the Blade and NightHunter paranormal romance series. Stephanie is a four-time nominee of the RITA® Award, the highest award in romance fiction. She has won many awards for her novels, including the prestigious Golden Heart® Award. She has received coveted starred reviews from Booklist, and Publishers Weekly has called her work "[a] genre-twister that will make readers...rabid for more." Stephanie also writes a thrilling romantic suspense series set in Alaska. Publisher's Weekly praised the series debut, ICE, as a "thrilling entry into romantic suspense," and Fresh Fiction called ICE an "edgy, sexy and gripping thriller." Equally as intense and sexy are Stephanie's contemporary romance novels, set in the fictional town of Birch Crossing, Maine. All of Stephanie's books, regardless of the genre, deliver the same intense, passionate, and emotional experience that has delighted so many readers.

www.stephanierowe.com

http://twitter.com/stephanierowe2

http://www.pinterest.com/StephanieRowe2/

https://www.facebook.com/StephanieRoweAuthor

Printed in Poland
by Amazon Fulfillment
Poland Sp. z o.o., Wrocław